BETHANY'S WELL

RENATA DAWN

Cover Design: by Stefan P.

Published by Strolling Donkeys, LLC, 30 N Gould St STE N, Sheridan, WY 82801

WWW.strollingdonkeys.com

Our mission is to help readers understand the importance of a personal relationship with Jesus Christ.

ISBN-13 979-8-9989104-8-7

❀ Formatted with Vellum

To Jesus Christ,
for guidance and discernment in my life.

CHAPTER 1

*R*osario House, November 2006

As I watched the flames rage through the open doorway with a heinous vengeance, I could swear I saw a shadow moving within the fire, near where Alma would have been. For a moment, it appeared to beckon her, and I could hear the faint sound of laughter. Was she being summoned to hell? Part of me wanted that to be true, and I'm glad she's dead. However, another part of me felt a flicker of sorrow over it. Helplessly, I watched as flames consumed the once-lovely Rosario House.

The heat intensified, and I began to back away, still mesmerized by the fire's beauty and destruction. Suddenly, I felt a hand grab my right arm and heard an all-too-familiar voice telling me to step back as the fire was spreading.

I turned to see Jasper, his face barely visible in the pitch-black night, lit only by the glow of the inferno. I held his gaze as I slowly backed away, pulling myself from the fire's overwhelming heat. My senses started to return, and I glanced around, panicking.

Jasper gripped my arm. "You need to leave immediately. I'll tell the authorities you weren't here."

I looked at him one last time as I stood there. "Where will you say I was tonight?"

He glanced around nervously. "I'll tell everyone you were at the cabin." Then he looked back at me. "I know it wasn't your fault what happened. She brought all this on herself. I don't want anyone trying to blame you for it. They may try to say she gave you a reason to hate her, and this is what happened. They're all dead now because of what she did."

I turned and walked toward my car, feeling numb. I could barely see anything except the dim light of the blaze. I found my car and got in. I drove away feeling alone, broken, and isolated, just as I did when I arrived some months ago. Things had only worsened since I came here.

I pulled out onto the main road and drove for a few minutes. I was slightly startled by the quickly approaching red flashing lights and deafening siren of a fire truck as it passed me. I realized how I had barely escaped with my life and just barely left before anyone could place me at the scene.

As I drove into the night, I began to realize I wasn't sorry for what happened to her. She killed herself. She killed all of them. She brought the worst out in me—the side I had always tried to suppress. I had a side that was similar to hers in many ways.

I prayed for the Lord to have mercy on her, as well as on me, for what had happened. Could I ever forgive her for what she had done? Could I forgive myself for stooping to her level? Perhaps now the murmuring and faint laughing would stop since I had left, just as it had begun when I arrived at this place. This is the place the locals call Bethany's Well.

I-10 From Florida to Arkansas

It had been a while since I had driven on the open road. I had always enjoyed driving on I-10 because it was relatively scenic in places and much slower-paced than many other interstates. I had the windows down, enjoying the warmer April weather.

I had left Miami to take a new archaeology job working on a pipeline survey, a phase one project, as opposed to the phase three full excavation I had just completed in downtown Miami. I had been recommended for this new project by a coworker from the Miami dig named Jeanette. She had been hired first and relocated here for immediate work at the end of our last project.

The sun was shining brightly, though it wasn't very hot this time of year. I started thinking about going swimming later if I arrived at the hotel before dark. I had never been to Arkansas before, so I was also looking forward to traveling and seeing more of the United States.

The drive was long, and as time passed, my enthusiasm began to wear off. I found myself wishing I were already there. I passed through Alabama and Mississippi—familiar places. My parents used to vacation in New Orleans a while back.

I regained some of my excitement as I crossed into Arkansas. The biggest change I noticed was that the trees grew taller and the wooded areas became denser. I loved the forest, so seeing this lifted my mood again. By nightfall, I arrived at the hotel. I was a little disappointed about missing the chance to swim, but at least I could settle in and get some rest. I had to be up early for work at 6:30 AM. The crew chief wanted to start early to get ahead of the heat.

When I checked in, I was told I didn't have a roommate assigned to my room. I was thrilled to have it to myself. The hotel was on the smaller side, but nice and surrounded by forest. It was located near a historical site, which I was eager to learn more about.

The room itself was small but cozy and clean. I liked it; it had a bit of old colonial charm. The hotel was an older two-story building with rooms that opened directly to the outside. There was a pool, along with picnic tables under the trees near the edge of the forest. There was also a community grill, which made me happy since I could cook steaks and hamburgers.

Suddenly, my cellphone rang.

"Hi, Calina, was your trip alright?" Jeanette asked.

"Yeah, it went fine," I told her. "I'm just getting ready for tomorrow."

She paused for a second, then casually asked, "Have you met Niles yet? The project director?"

"No, I haven't even heard from him," I said, adjusting the phone against my ear.

"Well," she replied, her voice dropping slightly, "he's weird."

"Weird how?" I asked.

She let out a short laugh. "He told me I wasn't a crew chief on his project, even though the company owner at Locate, Inc., hired me as one. Maybe it was a miscommunication or just egos clashing, but I don't like him already."

I could tell there was more under the surface. It surprised me a little—Jeanette seemed to hold grudges over things that felt a little petty. It was a side of her I hadn't really seen before.

That night, I lay in bed thinking about what I might do on the weekends to occupy my time. Maybe after work tomorrow, I could drive around, find a grocery store, and check out the local scene. I was also looking forward to meeting my new coworkers and seeing how this crew compared to the last one.

I drifted off to sleep, excited for what tomorrow would bring.

The next morning, my alarm woke me. I got dressed in cargo pants, leather boots, and a thin, long-sleeved cotton shirt. After applying sunscreen, I grabbed my bucket hat for sun protection and set my black backpack on the table. Inside were the essentials: extra sunscreen, a water bottle, the hat, and a plastic bag with toilet paper in case there weren't any restrooms out in the field.

I had packed a few granola bars and a bottle of Gatorade the night before. I figured I'd see what fruit the hotel offered to round out my lunch. Breakfast turned out to be simple: orange juice and cereal, with toast and hard-boiled eggs. I enjoyed the eggs and toast, and I grabbed a few bananas and apples to take with me before heading back to my room.

The morning air felt cool, but I knew it wouldn't last. By noon, it would be reasonably hot.

A large crowd had gathered in the parking lot, about thirty people in total. That's when I finally met Niles. He stepped forward and introduced himself to the group. To my surprise, he was nothing like I'd imagined based on Jeanette's description. He was actually kind of cute, with dark hair, blue eyes, and olive skin. Slim, but not exceptionally tall.

I was assigned to Jeanette's crew to start, and we loaded into the trucks to head out to the pipeline area. The site was surrounded by dense forest, thick with thorns and crawling with ticks. We were each handed a machete to help cut a path through the brush. Using compasses to guide our direction, we moved in a straight line through the undergrowth, stopping every thirty meters to dig shovel tests.

We arrived and started work at first light. The morning was cool, and I was grateful we had begun early, especially after seeing how dense the foliage was. After a while, I paused to take a water break and glanced around. Something felt off. Though my coworkers were scattered nearby, busy working, I had the unsettling sense that I was being watched. No one else was supposed to be out here—we were surveying for the oil pipeline, and the area had already been cleared.

I stood still for a moment, scanning the trees, but saw nothing out of place. Still, the feeling lingered. Shaking it off, I went back to work, though I couldn't shake the sensation that unseen eyes were tracking me.

By 11:30, we took our lunch break. The crew chief called out, "Alright, back to the trucks. Take thirty. Cool off and get out of the sun."

I climbed into one of the trucks, grateful for the air conditioning. I didn't really know anyone yet, so I kept to myself. There wasn't much to say anyway, other than the fact that I'd never been to Arkansas before and most of my fieldwork had been in phase three excavations. There were five other archaeologists besides me and the crew chief—friendly enough, but we were still strangers.

As the afternoon wore on, I focused on filling out shovel tests, logging the paperwork with a clipboard I kept in my backpack. The process moved quickly, and I kept a steady pace, ready for the day to end.

Around 2 PM, I checked my watch. The crew chief walked by and said, "Start packing up—we've got a half-hour drive back to the hotel."

Everyone looked relieved. The first day was behind us, and now I had a better idea of what to expect from the project. I'd also gotten a general introduction to the rest of the team.

Back at the hotel, I didn't waste time. I headed straight for the shower, then threw on fresh clothes and decided to find a grocery store. I considered asking the front desk for directions, but I decided to make an adventure out of it instead.

I got in the car and pulled onto the main road leading toward town. The drive was peaceful, lined with thick woods on both sides. After about fifteen minutes, I arrived in a small downtown area that looked like it hadn't changed much since the 1940s.

There was a town center with a small park and a statue of someone I didn't recognize. I made a mental note to look up who it was. Four large brick buildings surrounded the square, each housing old shops that looked like they had been there forever. As I drove past a small restaurant with a vintage sign and a warm glow inside, I thought to myself, *I'll have to try that place for lunch this weekend.*

I followed the main road, went halfway around the town square, and then continued straight. Just ahead, I spotted a grocery store and decided to stop. It was a smaller, older place, but it had a surprisingly wide selection of high-quality produce, along with a nice variety of lunch meats and ready-made soups. I picked up some milk, a hamburger patty, and a pack of buns —planning to grill out tomorrow night.

On the way back to the hotel, I passed a sign for Bethany's Well. I slowed down a little, reading it as I drove by. "Must be a historical site," I thought. "Maybe I'll check it out this weekend." I had already been planning to do some sightseeing, and that seemed like a good place to start.

When I pulled into the hotel parking lot, I noticed Jeanette's door was open. Carrying my groceries, I walked past and called out, "Hey, Jeanette."

She was inside with a few members of the crew, all gathered around a table, going over something.

"We're doing artifact inventory," she said without looking up. "These are from all four crews today. They'll be sent to the lab soon."

I nodded but couldn't help wondering why she hadn't mentioned any opportunity for overtime—or even asked if I'd be interested. Still, I smiled politely.

"I'm going to put these up. I'll see you all in the morning," I said, giving a quick wave to the not-so-interested group.

Back in my room, I put away the groceries, cooked dinner, and spent the rest of the evening making plans for tomorrow. I watched a little TV before heading to bed early.

The next morning, we gathered again for our daily debriefing. Niles ran through some safety protocols and gave us a bit more insight into the project.

"Some of you," he said, glancing around the group, "will be heading to a nearby phase three project pretty soon."

I perked up at that. Most of my experience was in phase three work, and I was genuinely excited at the idea of getting back to it.

The week passed quickly. As I got to know my crew better, I felt more comfortable and settled into the routine with each passing day. After work, I often drove around the area to explore a bit, usually stopping somewhere for a Coke. Each day, I passed that same sign for Bethany's Well, and with every glance, my curiosity grew.

The area's main historical attraction was a grand Victorian mansion, once owned by an oil tycoon during the Roaring Twenties. The oil industry had exploded here back then, giving rise to the town's name—Boom Town —a reflection of its oil boom past.

By Friday, I had made up my mind. "I'm going to see the mansion this weekend," I told myself, thinking about the ornate architecture and old stories it must hold. "And Bethany's Well, too."

I also remembered the little restaurant I'd seen in the town square. The mansion wasn't far from there, so I figured I could make a day of it.

I got back to the hotel and walked past Jeanette's room. Her door was open again, and no one was inside. She called out from the bathroom, saying they had left for the day.

I paused in the doorway. "Hey, would you want to come with me this weekend to check out some of the nearby sites?"

She stepped into view, towel-drying her hair. "Thanks, but I've already made plans. A few of us are going to a pow-wow."

I nodded, trying not to show my disappointment. "Oh, cool."

What bothered me wasn't that she had plans—it was that she hadn't thought to ask if I might want to come along too, especially since other crew members were going.

I headed back to my room, a little disheartened. Sitting on the edge of the bed, I realized I needed to make a greater effort to connect with the crew. If I were more open, I could find someone to hang out with over the weekend. Either way, I was still looking forward to getting out and exploring.

Tomorrow was Friday. One more day of work, and then I'd have the weekend to myself.

That evening, I kept it simple. I reheated some hamburger patties from the fridge, tossed them onto leftover buns, and finished off the rest of a bag of chips. As I ate, I caught myself wondering what it would be like to have a home and a husband—something I had never seriously considered until recently.

Friday morning came, and I felt a bit more energized. I got ready for work, excited that the weekend was almost here. The debriefing was brief, and we headed out early. The day grew hotter by the hour, but I was glad that most of the heavy work was finished before the worst of it hit.

After wrapping up a shovel test, I took a water break and leaned against a tree. That strange feeling crept over me again—the sense that I was being watched. I scanned the tree line, but nothing moved. Telling myself it was just my imagination, I turned to head toward my following test site.

That's when I heard it. A sharp snap—a branch breaking behind me.

I spun around. No one was there.

Heart pounding, I looked around again, this time a little more carefully. Still nothing. I tried to shake it off and quickly made my way to the next test, hoping to leave that unsettling area behind.

After work, I decided to drive around and unwind. I found myself near the town square and wandered into a charming antique store. There were a few pieces of furniture I liked, but as I admired a vintage dresser, I remembered—I didn't even have a house to put it in yet.

Feeling spontaneous, I walked across the street to Aurelio's Italian Restaurant, a place I had been eyeing all week. I ordered the country-fried steak with mashed potatoes and country gravy.

The restaurant was warm and inviting, with red and white checkered tablecloths, matching red chairs, and large front windows with red curtains that matched the tiled floor. It had the charm of an old diner, even without a counter.

The food was delicious, and as I finished my meal, I thought to myself, *I'll definitely come back here again.*

Walking back to my car, the loneliness crept in. I missed my friends and family more than I had expected. I loved being an archaeologist, but the solitude sometimes felt overwhelming without a crew to share the experience with.

Maybe I was starting to want more than just the following dig site. Perhaps I was beginning to enjoy a family of my own.

I returned to the hotel and set up my camping chair outside my room. The heat of the day had finally lifted, and the evening air felt comfortable. A few of the crew members were also sitting outside, scattered along the walkway in front of their rooms. We ended up talking about the project and sharing our experiences so far.

Everyone seemed to agree on one thing—they hated the heat and the thick foliage we had to cut through every day.

I chuckled and said, "An honorable archaeology death out here would be passing out from heat stroke, then getting eaten alive by ticks while lying unconscious in the brush."

They laughed, and for a moment, the tension eased. Still, I felt awkward. I struggled to find more to say, unsure of how to keep the conversation going.

I really wanted to make friends with the crew. I liked the project so far and hoped the awkwardness would fade with time.

CHAPTER 2

*A*fter sleeping in on Saturday morning, I got up feeling refreshed and decided to eat breakfast at the hotel. I planned to come back for a late lunch at the same restaurant after visiting the mansion. I was starving after the long week of hard work, so I ordered three boiled eggs with toast, a bowl of cereal, and a glass of orange juice.

I wore a lovely white eyelet sundress and a straw sunhat decorated with little plastic seashells. It was definitely more suited for the beach, but it was cute, and I liked it. I slipped on white sandals and grabbed my brown straw purse—also beach-themed, of course—before heading out.

There were no crew members around, and most of them were still sleeping in. I walked to my car, got in, and looked over the hotel's map of downtown. The mansion I wanted to visit was marked as a historic landmark, so I felt reasonably confident about where it was located.

Excited to be off on a little adventure, I pulled onto the road with the radio playing softly. I kept the windows up so my hat wouldn't blow off while driving. As I returned to the town square, I turned right at the roundabout, circling the statue and garden. The road was lined with a mix of small shops and old, stately homes—some Victorian, some colonial, and a few smaller cottages. It was a beautiful area, and as I took it all in, I began to think about having my own home someday.

"I want a little cottage," I murmured to myself, smiling at the thought. "With lots of gardens—flowers, vegetables, maybe even some fruit trees. And cats. Definitely cats."

Soon, I spotted the mansion up ahead and pulled into the parking lot. A lovely arched wooden sign in a soft shade of purple marked the entrance. As I got out and walked toward the front yard, I took in the sight of the massive Victorian home. Painted cream with accents of the same light purple as the sign, it had several turrets rising from the front, making it look like something out of a fairy tale. The yard was bursting with colorful flowers and roses of all shades. A ceramic birdbath stood in the middle, adorned with tiny carved hummingbirds.

I reached into my purse and pulled out a disposable camera, snapping a few photos of the vibrant garden and the ornate front porch. The porch was wide and welcoming, with hanging baskets full of flowers swaying gently in the breeze. White wrought-iron furniture—a few tables with matching chairs and several benches—invited visitors to sit and take it all in.

Walking up the steps, I reached the double front doors, painted in the same light purple hue. I pushed one open and stepped into a large foyer where tickets were sold. A woman behind the counter greeted me with a smile.

"Good morning," she said. "Admission is ten dollars."

I handed her the money and tucked my ticket into my purse as she continued.

"You're welcome to walk through the house at your own pace," she said. "And feel free to explore the backyard as well."

"Thank you," I replied, already glancing around, eager to explore.

I picked up a free brochure with information about the house and flipped through it as I wandered through the mansion. A painting in one of the hallways caught my eye—a man stood tall, dressed in a military uniform I didn't recognize, with a sword sheathed at his left side and his right hand resting on the hilt. The style suggested it was from another country, or maybe it held some esoteric symbolism I wasn't familiar with.

Next to him hung another portrait of two young women seated on a couch in elegant ball gowns. The brochure identified them as the daughters of Pierre Cormet, the man in the military uniform and the builder of the house.

My attention was drawn to the young woman on the right, dressed in a pale blue gown with sheer, matching sleeves. Her red hair was pulled up into a braided bun. There was something about her that unsettled me, as if I would come to dislike her despite the fact that she'd been dead for decades —long before I was ever born. Her name, according to the brochure, was Jocelynn Cormet.

I stood in front of her portrait, still thumbing through the brochure, when I suddenly gasped. One section described how the household—and a large part of the town—had died after drinking contaminated well water. The detail felt strangely out of place, ominous even. I looked back at Jocelynn's painted face, wondering what story she would tell if she could speak.

Moving on, I wandered into what looked like a living room and noticed French doors standing open. I stepped through them onto a back porch furnished with white wrought iron patio furniture. Beyond that was a beautiful garden, full of flowers, shaded by trees, and anchored by a graceful gazebo.

As I stood there, a heavy sadness seemed to settle over the space. The air felt thick, as if grief and remorse still lingered in the garden after all these years. A strange pressure crept into my chest, and I found myself wanting to leave—to get lunch, to explore the town square, anything to get away from that feeling.

I stepped back into the mansion, and the intensity faded slightly. Still, my thoughts lingered on what might have happened in this place. I wandered the house a bit longer before deciding to look for Bethany's Well and then grab lunch.

On my way out, I stopped at the ticket counter. The woman behind it looked up with a polite smile.

"Excuse me," I said. "Do you know how to get to Bethany's Well? And… do you like it? As far as landmarks go around here?"

She looked back at me with the strangest expression. "How did you even know about it?" she asked.

"I saw the sign for it off the main road into town—" I began, but before I could finish, a few people came in to buy tickets. I stepped to the side to wait for her, but after a few minutes, her glare toward me didn't fade. Feeling unwelcome, I just left.

As I headed to my car, I began to wonder how friendly the townsfolk really were. Starting the engine, I drove back down the main road out of town, looking for the sign again. When I spotted it, I turned off onto the side road. Ten minutes later, I came to another sign for Bethany's Well, turned right, and drove another five minutes.

The road ended at what looked like a small park. There was no real parking lot—just a patch of grass to pull onto and a wooden sign. I got out of the car and followed the arrow on the sign pointing toward a narrow path that resembled a nature trail.

I walked for a while until I came to a stone circle where a decayed well sat, its stones chaotic and upheaved. The place had an energy of grief and remorse that clung to the air. I raised my disposable camera, snapped a few photos, and kept moving down the trail.

The well left me disappointed. I had hoped for at least an information sign or some sort of history about the place. Instead, the trail led to a small, old, rustic cabin that looked as if pioneers had built it. Modern curtains hung in its window, which made me wonder if Bethany's Well was truly a landmark—or just a name for a private property, a business, or maybe even a summer camp.

I turned to leave, but as I walked back down the path, I heard faint murmuring from a man's voice. I stopped and looked around. No one. The hairs on the back of my neck rose; I felt the same eerie sense of being watched that I'd felt a few times at work that week.

I lifted my camera and snapped a photo in the direction of the sound. The murmuring shifted into faint laughing. I took another picture. Then, to my right, a twig snapped.

I spun and raised the camera again, snapping another shot. The feeling of a presence grew stronger, almost pressing in on me now. More whispers drifted through the trees—two male voices this time, speaking to each other and laughing occasionally as if sharing some private joke.

My heart thudded. I picked up my pace, hurrying down the path, the sound of their whispering still following me as I went.

I felt an unexpected intensity behind me, as if someone were standing just out of sight. I spun around, heart pounding, fully expecting to see someone or something there. But the path was empty.

Without hesitating, I ran toward my car, jumped in, and locked the doors. My hands shook as I started the engine. I pulled out of the grass lot and sped off, the forest quickly vanishing in my rearview mirror. Shaken, I stopped at the main road to catch my breath and gather my thoughts.

With nowhere else to be and no one to report to, I decided to head back into town for lunch. It was also a good time to get the film developed from the camera.

I parked in front of Aurelio's Italian Restaurant in the town square, but I didn't get out right away. I sat in the car, hands pressed to the steering wheel, feeling the weight of what had just happened. The whole experience had been more traumatic than I realized.

Eventually, I made my way inside and ordered lunch. I thought about keeping it light, but after everything, I needed something comforting. I ordered a cheeseburger with French fries and a Coke. Usually, I would have gone with a salad, but today was an exception. The Coke tasted especially good—sharp and cold.

I took my time eating, staring out the large front window in front of me. Across the street, I noticed a drugstore and decided I'd take the film there once I finished eating. Having a plan gave me a little spark of enthusiasm. I finished my meal, left a tip for the waitress, and stepped back outside.

Crossing through the small park in the center of the square, I passed by potted flowers and colorful, blooming bushes. Cement benches faced a large statue, and I walked over to get a closer look. A plaque beneath it read: *Pierre Cormet.*

He stood tall in a three-piece suit, narrow silhouettes defining his frame. His face looked peaceful, proud. According to the brochure I'd read earlier, Cormet had made his fortune by discovering oil on his land. He had poured that wealth into the town—Boomtown—funding the schoolhouse, the library, and even the church to my right, just past the square.

The Hands of God, it was called. After dropping off the film, I decided I'd walk over and check the hours on the sign out front.

I continued toward the drugstore. The building had an old-fashioned brick facade, untouched by modern renovations. Like the rest of the town square, it felt like stepping into a preserved past.

I smiled slightly. Any archaeologist would appreciate this glimpse into history—into how things once were, in this quiet corner of the world.

I crossed the street after waiting for a few cars to pass and stepped into the drugstore. The building was old, with a faint musty smell lingering in the air. I glanced around until I spotted the photo department to the left, then made my way over to scan the pricing options based on return time.

I chose the one-week return, filled out the envelope with my information, placed the disposable camera inside, sealed it, and handed it to the man behind the counter. Payment would be due once the film was developed and the photos were ready for pickup.

After that, I walked back toward the church and stopped to read the sign out front. The Sunday morning service was listed at 9:30 AM. I made a mental note and took a moment to admire the building. It was made of stone with several arched stained-glass windows—beautiful and unique. Clearly, the Cormet family had lived well and had good taste in architecture. Red roses bordered the front of the church, vibrant against the soft gray stone.

I returned to my car, debating whether to head straight back to the hotel or take a short drive out of town just to explore. Curiosity won out. I pulled onto the main road and drove for a while. More forest stretched ahead—tall trees and soft, rolling green. It was peaceful, the kind of landscape that invited deep breaths and quiet thoughts.

Eventually, I came to a small park and decided to stop. I got out and walked along a nature trail, letting my mind wander to tomorrow's plans. I decided to attend the church service in the morning and explore the historical building a bit further. At least it was something local to do.

The wind rustled through the trees, sending leaves fluttering gently to the ground. It was a beautiful spring afternoon. After a few minutes, I headed back to the car, planning to grab a Coke on the way to the hotel and rest for a while. I could take a swim later, maybe watch some TV, or catch a movie if anything was playing nearby.

The drive back to the hotel was beautiful, with sunshine filtering through the surrounding woods. I stopped at a convenience store, bought a

Coke, and headed on. When I arrived, the parking lot was quiet; no one from the crew seemed to be around. I decided I'd spend the rest of the day at the pool.

The pool was small and tucked behind the hotel, hidden from the road so no one passing by could see who was swimming. I slipped into the water and floated on my back, letting the coolness soothe me as I thought about the day. My eyes drifted shut, and when I opened them again, the sky had deepened toward dusk. My fingers were wrinkled from the water. I must have been in there longer than I realized, but that was fine. It had been a long time since I'd had the chance to swim.

Later, I went back to my room, put on a movie, and tried to relax. The film didn't hold my interest, and before long, I drifted off to sleep.

In my dream, a lovely young woman appeared. She had long, wavy black hair, but I couldn't see her face. She wore a burgundy dress and stood beside Bethany's Well—but in the dream, the well was whole, in perfect condition. I sensed she was young, maybe fourteen. She felt happy and sweet-natured but lonely, wishing she had friends. Her father and brother had built the cabin next to the well. She spun and danced in the breeze, her long hair flowing as the sunlight glimmered around her.

This dream felt unlike any I'd had before. I was aware I was dreaming. Then, suddenly, I sensed someone walking up behind the girl—a dark figure, ancient and cunning, his purpose steeped in deceit. The realization jolted me awake.

I lay there, heart pounding, staring at the dim room. It was 3:33 AM. Movement caught my eye—a shadow passing across the narrow gap in the curtains, cast by the lights on the outside walkway. The same feeling I'd had in the woods returned, that prickling sensation of being watched.

I got up, closed the curtains tightly, and turned on the lamp beside the bed. With the light on, I climbed back under the covers and tried to sleep. I set my alarm for 7:30 AM so I'd have time to get ready for church. I planned to go out for breakfast in the morning.

I had a hard time falling back asleep, and by the time my alarm finally went off, I felt groggy and tired. I turned it off but stayed in bed a little longer, only realizing after fifteen minutes that I needed to get moving. I got up and dressed quickly, choosing a long black skirt and a short-sleeved, black-and-white polka dot blouse—business attire but still comfortable. I slipped on black sandals, wanting to keep my feet cool in the growing heat.

I jumped into my car and headed toward the restaurant I'd seen near the mansion the day before. The sign outside had read *Momma's Kitchen—Breakfast and Lunch,* and I was drawn to its cozy, bohemian charm. The building resembled an old house, complete with a front porch and an upstairs balcony dining area.

I made it there before 9:00 AM. It wasn't busy yet, and the hostess must've noticed I was in a hurry. She pointed me toward the counter service: a small pastry and coffee section separate from the main dining area. I chose a coconut and chocolate donut and a chocolate donut with sprinkles. While waiting, I browsed the menu, which was printed on simple paper and stacked for customers to take on their way out. I added a hot vanilla chai tea to my order.

I decided I'd definitely come back for lunch after church.

The donuts were fantastic. The chocolate icing was rich, almost like fudge, and the tea was smooth and not overly sweet—perfect alongside the donuts. I picked a table by the front window, painted a deep red, with matching chairs. The table beside mine was stained a dark espresso color, and another nearby was bright yellow with rose-colored chairs. A cozy couch sat to the left of the counter area, which served more like a small coffee shop tucked inside the larger restaurant.

Momma's Kitchen offered two distinct vibes under one roof: counter service with pastries and drinks, and a full sit-down restaurant. I really liked it here. I could already tell this was going to become one of my favorite spots.

CHAPTER 3

I looked at my watch and realized I had only five minutes to get to church. I hurried out, got into my car, and drove the short distance. Pulling into the front guest parking off the street, I headed toward the gorgeous engraved wooden double doors at the entrance.

As soon as I stepped inside, I heard music playing. I found myself in a large foyer, but the sanctuary doors closed just as I walked over to enter. The foyer itself was striking, with colorful tile flooring and a skylight of stained glass overhead.

When I finally stepped into the sanctuary, I was surprised by how open and large it was. Arched stained-glass windows lined the walls, and the tall ceiling held rows of chandeliers. Wooden pews with built-in cushions filled the space, all set on light rose-colored carpet. I slipped into a pew at the back while the congregation stood and sang.

The music was beautiful, and I enjoyed listening to it. A lady sitting in the corner to my left noticed me and smiled. After the song ended and everyone sat down for announcements, she greeted me. I returned the smile and said hello. The pastor announced a church potluck and cookout for next weekend to kick off summer. I made a mental note to check it out.

When the sermon began, I listened closely. It was interesting, though difficult to follow since I didn't know much about the Bible. After the service ended, I stepped back outside and realized it was only 10:40. Too early for lunch, and I didn't want to go back to the hotel just yet. I remembered spotting a bookstore near the drugstore and decided to walk over, though I didn't want to be gone too long with my car still parked at the church.

The bookstore looked small from the outside. I pushed open the pink front door, and a bell chimed above me as I entered. Inside, it was warm and inviting, with hardwood floors and bookshelves stretching from floor to ceiling. In one corner, an archway made entirely of stacked books caught my eye. I thought it was adorable.

I wandered over to the religion section, thumbed through the Bibles, and eventually chose one. After debating for a few minutes, I decided to buy it. With the book tucked under my arm, I returned to my car and started driving with no real destination in mind.

After a while, I reached another small town. Spotting a grocery store, I decided it was a good time to get my weekly shopping done. Luckily, the hotel offered washing machines and sold small packets of detergent. I picked up a variety of fruits, including grapes, apples, bananas, peaches, and tangerines, as well as granola bars and trail mix. I added bottled water, juice boxes for work, and a box of sandwich bags to my cart before heading to check out.

I wanted to get milk and orange juice, but I thought I already had *that at the hotel.*

I purchased my groceries and brought everything back. As I arrived, I noticed Jeanette's door was open. It struck me as odd for a Sunday afternoon, but then I figured she might have crew members visiting. As I walked past, I heard her call out, "Hey!"

I stopped and looked in. Jeanette was sitting with a few of the crew, chatting animatedly about the pow-wow they had attended. I had honestly forgotten they were going.

"So, what did you do this weekend?" she asked, half expecting me to say I'd just stayed at the hotel.

"I went to see the local mansion," I said, "and also Bethany's Well."

Jeanette raised an eyebrow. "Bethany's Well? What's that supposed to be?"

"It's a landmark I found," I explained. "There's a sign for it on the main road."

She frowned. "There's no sign on the main road for a place like that."

I shook my head. "You must have missed it. There's no way I would've found an old well otherwise."

She stared at me for a moment as though I had made a mistake, then turned back to the others. The crew began talking about their trip—how they'd driven over three hours after work on Friday, gotten a hotel room for two nights, and made a whole weekend out of it. I was glad they'd had fun.

After chatting for a few minutes, I excused myself to put away my groceries. Remembering the Bible I'd left in my car, I went back for it as well.

Later, I decided to go swimming before heading to Momma's Kitchen for a late lunch—or an early dinner. The water was pleasant, warmed by the sun. Floating on my back, I thought again about Jeanette's claim that there weren't any signs for Bethany's Well. Perhaps she was distracted by driving or lost in thought and overlooked it.

The thought made me even more eager to see the pictures once they were developed. I wondered if the camera could really capture anything strange—if there was anything there at all. I suppose I'd find out soon enough.

I stayed in the pool until my hands turned prune-like, then went in to shower. Afterward, I towel-dried my hair and decided to let the rest air dry. I slipped into an olive green sundress with tan leather sandals and headed out. Passing Jeanette's open door again, I peeked in and saw her still talking with the others. Things had felt a little frosty between us lately, but I told myself it was fine. She probably just had more in common with them. And maybe that would give me the chance to meet new people, too.

I went back to Momma's Kitchen for an early dinner and to relax. The house itself was painted in an array of colors—the exterior teal, the trim around the windows red, and the siding a deep violet. Yellow curtains hung in the windows, matching the yellow patio tables and chairs, while the indoor tables and chairs were olive green, just like the front door. Potted plants in colorful ceramic planters lined the porch, and clear string lights were strung across the balcony and railing for night dining.

The hostess greeted me and led me through the front coffee counter into the dining room. It was cozy, with an old brick fireplace centered between two sets of French doors. She seated me at a faded yellow table by the fireplace and handed me a menu. After looking it over, I decided on meatloaf with mashed potatoes and gravy, along with another vanilla chia tea.

The food was delicious, but I couldn't shake the pang of sadness that came with eating alone. I hoped that would change soon. Maybe I could even think about buying a house in the near future. I ate slowly, taking my time, since the restaurant wasn't crowded. After finishing, I paid the bill, left a tip, and headed back to my car.

Back at the hotel, I flipped through some brochures of local attractions. Rosario Mansion caught my attention, as did Cormet's Cave. I decided to save those outings for next weekend, with one on Saturday and the other on Sunday, which was the church potluck.

I spent the rest of the evening alternating between preparing for work and resting while watching TV. At one point, I picked up the Bible I had bought and thumbed through it, making plans to start reading more seriously after work during the week.

When bedtime came, I set my alarm for 6:30 AM, slept relatively peacefully, and got up early to get dressed and eat breakfast before heading to the morning briefing. Then I joined my crew for shovel testing.

The week passed uneventfully, the job slipping into a steady routine. Most evenings, I came back to the hotel, made dinner, and read from the Bible. Jeanette continued offering overtime to the same few people, so I mostly kept to myself.

By Friday, I overheard that the crew was planning to go to a local bar. Jenny stopped by my room and asked if I wanted to join.

"They're not going to drink," she explained. "Just to play pool."

"I don't know how to play," I admitted.

She smiled. "That's okay. I can help you learn on Saturday night."

I agreed, hoping it might be fun and maybe a chance to get to know the crew better, finally.

After work, I thought about my film and when I should pick it up tomorrow. I wanted to visit the cave and maybe go to the bar to play pool. I decided I'd head to the cave in the morning, then swing by to get the film afterward. Playing pool felt optional. If I saw some of the crew around in the evening, I'd join them, but if not, it wasn't that important.

Back at the hotel, I debated what to do for dinner. Grilling a steak and baking a potato sounded like a great combination. I drove to the grocery store for my weekly shopping and added a steak, a potato, and a small container of butter to my cart. Just before checkout, I thought about what to drink and grabbed a two-liter of Coke. The hotel had ice, and I wanted to eat in more this weekend.

When I returned, I grilled the steak and cooked the potato in the microwave. The meal was delicious; I loved the steak. As I ate, I thought about the potluck at church on Sunday and what I could bring. I realized I should have picked something up at the grocery store, but I had forgotten. Maybe I could grab cookies at the drugstore tomorrow.

After dinner, I read from the Bible and prayed for a while. Then I sat out front in my camping chair, sipping Coke and watching people come and go. Jenny came back from dinner out and waved. She always seemed cheerful, mature, and like she had her life together.

Eventually, I decided to head to bed so I'd be rested for the cave trip in the morning. As I drifted off to sleep, my mind returned to thoughts of the film and what it might reveal.

In my dream, I was in a classroom—a large schoolroom with white walls painted over wooden boards. The same young girl I had seen before sat at a desk, her back turned toward me, her hair falling straight down. She had swiveled around in her chair, whispering to the friend behind her.

The young girl noticed a new student sitting at the back of the room. The newcomer had long red hair, which the girl thought was pretty. She smiled at her. Her friend kept whispering, but the young girl noticed the red-haired girl looking back at her, so she smiled again. This time, the new girl didn't return the smile. Instead, her expression hardened into a menacing glare. The young girl quickly turned back around, avoiding her eyes.

I jolted awake, knowing this wasn't just a dream. It felt more like someone's memory, something that had really happened. I couldn't shake the sense that something was brewing for that poor young girl.

Eventually, I drifted back to sleep and woke naturally after having slept in. It felt good to rest after a long week of shovel tests. I headed to the hotel lobby for breakfast and chose toast with peanut butter and milk. Craving something sweet, I added a bowl of cereal. I also took a few hard-boiled eggs and some fruit back to my room, along with another small container of milk. I decided to make a salad later with the bagged greens and honey mustard dressing I had, and the eggs would go perfectly in it.

After dropping the food off, I got in my car and left for the cave. The day was sunny, and the drive was pleasant. Still, my mind circled back to the dream. It wasn't just a dream; it had started after I arrived here. This place had a dark history, and somehow, I felt I was being drawn into it.

When I arrived at the cave, I parked near a small building that served as a ticket booth, gift shop, and restroom. Inside, I joined the short ticket line and paid twelve dollars for admission. With ticket in hand, I walked toward the cave entrance, where a small line had already formed. The tour guide checked our tickets and asked where we were all from. The group was a mix of locals and visitors from across the country.

While waiting, I glanced through the brochure for Cormet's Cave. As the name suggested, the Cormet family had funded the site's opening. The cave had been discovered on their land, and in 1962, they opened it to the public.

We sat on metal benches for about five more minutes until the guide gathered us together and led us inside. The temperature dropped immediately, and the damp air wrapped around us. Lights strung along the walls illuminated our path, casting long shadows across the stone.

We came to a bridge spanning a vast chasm. The space beside it was lit, revealing the jagged, haphazard holes pockmarking the floor. I imagined how treacherous it must have been for the first explorers, navigating this place with only a lantern in hand. The stillness pressed in, calming yet unsettling. Out here, in the slow breath of stone and water, nature existed untouched, indifferent to the hurried pace of the world above.

I could tell we were taking a route that circled back to the front entrance. Once we stepped out, it took a few minutes for my eyes to fully adjust to the sunlight again. I found myself more excited about seeing the developed film than I had been about visiting the cave. I was eager to pick it up now.

I drove back toward the town square. The drive was a little long but pleasant, lined with woods and historic homes that passed by my window.

When I arrived at the drugstore, I went straight inside to pick up the long-awaited film. Remembering I wanted cookies, I stopped at the snack aisle first. I picked out Oreos and chocolate chip cookies, then headed to the photo department to pay for everything.

Finally, the pictures were ready. The envelope with the developed film was slipped into a sack, and I paid before hurrying out of the store. I rushed to my car, eager to open the envelope.

At first, the photos looked normal, and a wave of disappointment began to sink in. I had been so sure something would show up. Then I froze, staring at one photo of the well—the exact spot where I had heard the two male voices laughing and talking.

In the picture, a faint image appeared: a long face staring back at me. It seemed to have horns, though only the bases were visible at the top of the head. The male figure had an inhuman-looking nose, large and sharply angled downward. Its eyes were fixed directly on me. Beside it, a second male faced the first, resembling him with the same prominent nose and horns.

That was all the camera had caught—just their faces. But at least now I knew I wasn't imagining things. Something had been there.

Then I turned another photo and saw the most bizarre image I had ever encountered. A woman—or something shaped like one—stood by the well. She wore all gray clothing and a long gray head covering. Her skin looked gray, too. The head covering shadowed most of her face except for her chin. She was tall and slim, her stance haunting and foreboding, as though she were part of the dark history of Bethany's Well itself.

I set the pictures down, took a moment to think, and then decided to drive back to the hotel. On the way, I looked for the sign that had led me to Bethany's Well, but saw nothing. Jeanette's words crept into my mind. Maybe there was no sign at all. Maybe something was meant for me to find that place. Perhaps it wasn't a local landmark after all.

CHAPTER 4

$\mathcal{I}$ rested in my hotel room until the evening, waiting to go out with the crew. I didn't want to leave too close to the time, but I had promised some of them I would join, so I went. I put on a jean skirt, a floral blouse, and sandals, leaving my hair down.

Everyone was meeting at a bar, so I drove to the town square, parked, and went inside. Spotting some of the crew, I walked over to greet them. Jenny chatted with me briefly before moving on to engage with others. Once more people arrived, the crew started a pool game. No one showed me how to play as they had promised, and it was clear they wanted to win. I quickly lost interest and felt disappointed in them.

Across the bar, at another pool table, I noticed a guy watching me. He was tall and thin, with hazel eyes and dark brown hair—nice looking. I didn't usually get much attention from men, so I glanced back at him every so often.

My focus shifted to him rather than the poor game of pool. I was ready to sit out the next round anyway. After a while, he came over and suggested where I should aim my shot. I smiled and followed his advice.

Toward the end of the evening, he returned and asked for my phone number. Instead, I told him I would take his. He found a scrap of paper, wrote down his name and number, and handed it to me with a smile before I left with the rest of the crew.

Back at the hotel, I declined an invitation to a local club some of them were heading to. I didn't care for the taste of alcohol anyway. Why bother when there had already been a perfectly good bar? Maybe they wanted something livelier—there hadn't been many people at the bar, and it had been quiet.

Later, I went to bed, looking forward to church in the morning. I drifted off to sleep and woke the next day feeling refreshed. I dressed, ate breakfast, grabbed the cookies I'd bought, and headed to church. This time, I arrived earlier but still chose a seat in the back. I enjoyed the singing and the music.

Everyone sat down for the sermon, and the preacher began to tell a story. He said he had once been called at two in the morning, many years ago, by a man pleading for him to come to his home. When he arrived, the man begged him to pray for his salvation.

The man confessed that he knew he had wasted his chances to follow God, but now he felt as though his legs were on fire. He was sick and believed he would soon die, certain he was going to hell. Desperate, he pleaded with the pastor to pray for him, convinced that the Lord would hear the pastor's prayers.

The pastor described how the man screamed in agony, insisting the fire was rising through his body. He cried out that he smelled sulfur, that the flames were consuming him, and still he begged for prayer. The pastor prayed, and although the man initially continued to argue with him, the burning sensation eventually faded. The smell of sulfur left. Peace replaced the terror. The man knew that God had heard the pastor's prayers and that he had been given one last chance to be saved.

The preacher explained that the man didn't die from the illness he had at the time. Instead, God completely transformed his life.

After the sermon, I followed the crowd into the recreation area of the church, a large gym set up with tables and chairs. At the far end, a long buffet line stretched across several tables, filled with dishes the congregation had prepared. I placed my cookies at the dessert table near the end of the line.

The pastor came in, prayed, and blessed the meal. Then the crowd began moving through the line, filling their plates. I liked that he prayed over the food, but I wasn't very hungry. I took a couple of biscuits, covered them in sausage gravy, and found a place to sit, planning to go back for more later.

Not long after, a lady and her family sat beside me. They were friendly, asking questions about me: where I was from, and what I did for a living. Later, I went back for seconds, grabbing a can of Coke before returning for dessert. The lady introduced herself as Lydia, and before she left, she gave me her phone number. I gave her mine as well, glad to have made a friend at church.

I decided to rest back at my room and planned to stop by Bethany's Well again on the way back. When I tried to find the sign, it was gone. Still, I remembered where the turn was and drove there by memory. Parking on the grass again, I got out and looked around. As I passed the well, I began to hear the same whispering and faint laughing as before.

I stepped closer and peered over the stone wall. Suddenly, a shadow figure rushed up from behind me, and I felt a hard shove against my back. My chin scraped painfully against the jagged edge of a stone, one section missing where the rock had broken away.

I steadied myself and glanced inside the well. There was nothing but darkness, with only the faintest shimmer at the bottom that might have been water. Turning quickly, I started back toward my car. That's when I heard my name; this time, called by a woman's voice.

I spun around, but no one was there. Heart racing, I hurried back to my car, dug in the console for a Band-Aid, and pressed it over the scrape on my chin.

Back at the hotel, I couldn't shake the feeling that something was happening at Bethany's Well. I had no one to confide in about the strange events, which left me both discouraged and restless. Feeling lonely and bored, I thought of the man from the bar. Maybe I could at least distract myself. If he came across as odd, I would simply hang up and block his number.

I found the slip of paper he'd given me in my purse. His name, *Trevor*, was written neatly across the top, followed by his number. His handwriting was elegant—I hadn't noticed before. I hadn't planned on calling him, but curiosity stirred out of nowhere, and I gave in.

When he answered, I hesitated before telling him who I was. We talked for a while. He mentioned he was studying to become a life insurance agent, and I shared that I was an archaeologist working on a pipeline survey in town.

Then he asked if I wanted to go out for dinner. I wasn't sure, but he offered to pick me up at the hotel in thirty minutes. Against my better judgment, I agreed—if only for the experience of going on an actual date. I still didn't know if I liked him.

He arrived on time, and I walked out to his vehicle. Sliding into the passenger seat, I heard him ask, "Where would you like to go for dinner?"

"Aurelio's," I said. It was close by, and I knew the place. I picked it instead of Momma's Kitchen, my real favorite, because if the date went badly, I didn't want anyone I knew seeing us there and remembering it the next time I went in to eat.

We went in and looked over the menu. I ordered a cheeseburger and fries with a Coke, while Trevor chose meatloaf and mashed potatoes. As we waited, he told me he had a father and a sister in town but was estranged from his mother, who had been abusive when he was growing up. I didn't know what to say; it felt awkward for him to share something so personal so soon.

He went on to say he liked art and that it had been his favorite subject in school. Still, he painted a disheartening picture of his life. According to him, he didn't go to church or do anything to better himself.

After dinner, he dropped me off at the hotel and asked if he could come up. I told him no, thanked him for the meal at Aurelio's Restaurant, and wished him good night. I didn't expect to hear from him again.

Back in my room, I got ready for the next morning. I spent the rest of the evening reading the Bible, watching a little TV, and praying. I hoped the week would pass quickly and that I could learn more about Bethany's Well soon. Eventually, I fell asleep, only to be woken by the sound of my alarm, signaling another workweek.

I got ready, went to the lobby for breakfast, and then headed to the morning debriefing. Niles seemed annoyed and began discussing the crew chiefs he had hired. Everyone noticed he left Jeanette out of the list. It was obvious something was going on behind the scenes, and whatever it was, things weren't good between Niles and Jeanette.

I was assigned to Jeanette's crew for the week. Right away, I noticed she wasn't the same as when I had known her in Miami. Now she acted as if everything she did was superior to everyone else's. I ignored it and focused on my shovel test, just trying to get through the day.

The week passed uneventfully until Friday, when Jeanette called a meeting for her crew. She was furious that we weren't making the progress she expected, though I had no idea why—everyone was working. Jenny headed back to the last spot where she'd been digging, and Jeanette snapped at the rest of us to get back to work "like Jenny," lacing her command with profanity.

Jenny overheard it through the walkie-talkies. Later, she came over to apologize. "I was just tired of hearing Jeanette complain," she said. "I didn't mean to make you all look bad."

I told her it was okay, that she hadn't done anything wrong. "It's Jeanette," I said. "She's the one in the wrong for acting like that in the first place."

I knew something was going on with the crew, as I was switched without being asked if it was okay. When we returned to the hotel, Jeanette went straight over to Niles's friends and the other crew chiefs, bragging about how far she had gotten that day. The truth was that she didn't do any shovel tests herself. She filled out the paperwork and scouted ahead of us to assess the conditions and determine if shovel testing was feasible. I thought she should have given credit to her crew for the progress instead of claiming it for herself.

Jenny overheard her and muttered to me, "I'm not letting another boss of mine cuss at me again."

The more I saw, the more I realized Jeanette burned bridges with people over time. I guess I hadn't really known her in Miami, since I had only started talking to her toward the end of that project. Back then, we mostly discussed negative situations with the crew, which involved people I didn't get along with. Now I wondered if part of the problem had been me. Maybe I had my own issues and negativity to work through. Maybe I gossiped too much about people I didn't care for. I began to notice aspects of my behavior that I no longer liked.

In the evenings, I spent a little time talking with Trevor each night. I noticed I had stopped reading the Bible as much since meeting him. I didn't feel serious about him, but at the same time, I wasn't sure if I would meet anyone else soon—someone who might want a family and a home the way I did. I worried I was putting too much pressure on Trevor to be all the things I wanted, which was part of the reason I invited him to join me and some of the crew for dinner at Aurelio's Kitchen.

It seemed like a good chance to get to know him without being alone together, and to see how he was with other people. He arrived shortly after I did, which was fortunate since he wouldn't have known anyone otherwise. We sat down, looked over the menu, and talked. I felt like trying something different, so I ordered the chicken fingers with barbecue dipping sauce and French fries.

During the meal, I noticed Trevor making small talk with a pretty girl from the crew named Kirsten. I wasn't jealous, but I couldn't help wondering about his loyalty and how serious he was about me. He paid her more attention than I expected, and I could tell Kirsten noticed. She seemed uncomfortable with it, and I began to feel I was right not to get too attached to him.

I ordered a personal pan pizza and a Coke. I noticed Trevor's attention turning back to me again, and at the end of dinner, he paid for my meal once more. When we left, he asked if he could come back to the hotel to see me afterward. I agreed, but only for a few minutes, using the excuse that it was a workday tomorrow.

He came up to my room and leaned in, wanting to kiss me. I could tell where he hoped things would lead, so I told him I needed to go to sleep and that he should leave. He lingered for a while, but I stood firm in my refusal. Eventually, he left, though I could sense hard feelings behind it.

The next morning, at the briefing, Jenny caught me before things started. "I think Trevor is good-looking," she said, giving me a grin. "Is he smart?"

"I don't know him well enough yet to say," I answered. I got the feeling she was a little interested in him, even though she had a boyfriend. It made me wonder if maybe people weren't as loyal to the ones they were dating as I had once believed.

After that, I began focusing more on rereading the Bible and less on Trevor. I figured he was looking for casual relationships before marriage anyway. I thought about spending the weekend by myself, checking out the other mansion I hadn't seen yet. I also wanted to go to church and spend some time with God.

On Friday, Trevor called and asked me to go out to dinner after work. I agreed, and he insisted on picking me up. As we drove to Aurelio's Restaurant, he had the windows down.

"My car's air conditioner is broken," he said. "I don't have the money to fix it right now. You know, passengers can chip in too."

I stayed quiet and ignored the comment.

He shifted the conversation. "So, how's Kirsten doing?"

"She's okay," I replied, then glanced at him. "Why do you always ask about her? You've only met her once."

A coy smile spread across his face. "She's nice."

I didn't believe that for a second. I knew what he really meant—he thought she was pretty. That was why he asked.

I ordered the chicken fingers again; this time, we mainly ate in silence. Afterward, he drove me back to the hotel and asked once more to come up to my room. Instead, I suggested we sit and talk at the pool. He agreed, though reluctantly.

Once we sat down, he started talking about a comedy show he liked to watch on TV. I decided to ask him directly where he saw things going with us.

He looked at me for a moment. "I'd like to marry someone like you," he said, "but I don't know if I want to marry you."

I asked if I could meet some of his friends or family. He shook his head. "Whenever I introduce girls to my family, that's when things start to fall apart."

As he talked more, I began to notice how much he spoke about his mother and how she had treated him, and how both of his serious relationships had ended with his ex-girlfriends doing him wrong. Listening to him,

I realized he needed to care about how he treated people if he wanted good people to stay in his life.

After everything he said, I knew he wasn't the hope I had once thought he might be for a husband. I excused myself for the night, and he left. Relief washed over me as soon as he was gone.

I couldn't make things happen just because I wanted them to. I couldn't turn someone into what they weren't. Trevor was who he was, and he had been telling me all along about himself and what he wanted. I simply hadn't been listening—blinded by my own immaturity and lack of experience, believing I could change a person. But I knew now that only God could change people.

CHAPTER 5

That night, I fell asleep and slipped back into the dream of the young woman with the long black hair. She was sitting in her classroom again. However, her desk had been moved this time; it now faced north instead of east.

Across the room, another girl was whispering to the new student, a red-haired girl, about someone she disliked. From the description, it was clear she was speaking about the girl with the long black hair.

When the dismissal bell rang, the two walked out together. As they passed, the girl with black hair heard her own name called. *Bethany.* So it had been about her after all. She also listened to the red-haired girl's name—*Jocelynn.*

Bethany went home and told her mother what had happened. Her mother urged her to ignore the cruelty of her classmates. It was her last year of primary school, after all, and soon she would be able to move on to high school. Few students in 1890 made it that far, but her mother wanted her to get an education. She believed it would bring Bethany success in life.

I woke with the sting of Bethany's hurt still lingering inside me. She felt betrayed by her new classmates, and she wished she had never come to this school or this town. I understood her. I had dealt with bullies, too. And I was starting to see a pattern. Jocelynn seemed rich, popular, and influential.

She used it to wound others, perhaps out of malice, perhaps out of her own unresolved trauma.

Shaking off the dream, I got dressed and decided to head out for breakfast at Momma's Kitchen before visiting the Rosario Mansion. The morning drive into town was peaceful, the air warming as the sun rose higher. Trevor hadn't texted me that morning, but I didn't mind. The silence felt like a relief.

At the restaurant, I ordered my favorite breakfast: strawberry pancakes with whipped cream and an unsweetened iced tea, and sat near the fireplace again; this time, at an olive-green table. When I finished, I paid, left a tip, and set off toward the Rosario Mansion.

The drive took about fifteen minutes before I reached a tall metal gate framed by substantial stone walls that surrounded the property. Off to the right, I noticed a smaller Victorian home with a similar style to the much larger mansion looming ahead. Pulling into a small parking lot, I parked the car and walked up to the entrance.

The mansion was painted off-white, and I could tell it had been repainted—the intricate woodwork and paneling looked refreshed. Several turrets rose from the structure, much like the ones I had seen at Cormet Mansion.

Stepping inside, I immediately preferred this place over Cormet's. The entrance opened into a ticket counter, as well as a beautiful Victorian-themed gift shop. Displayed inside were delicate jewelry, hand mirrors with matching combs, and an array of hair accessories and clothespins. A few Victorian-style dresses and shoes were for sale as well, along with scarves.

I wandered the shop for nearly thirty minutes before even buying a ticket. There was also a tea room, offering lunch, light snacks, and a traditional tea service for visitors who wanted the whole experience.

Finally, I purchased my fifteen-dollar ticket and stepped into the mansion itself. The foyer was grand, with oak floors and tall paneled walls. Though the walls had been repainted off-white, they seemed a little dull compared to the intricate wooden details, which deserved more emphasis.

As I moved through the lavish rooms, a prickle crept over me—as if someone were watching. I glanced around, but none of the other guests, scattered quietly among the halls, seemed to be paying me any attention.

Then I heard it—the faint sound of laughing and whispering. It followed me into a room with a black grand piano, several dark blue couches patterned with white flowers, and a bar area. Clearly, this space was used for events. But I couldn't shake the sensation of unseen eyes fixed on me.

My pace quickened, and I moved through the rest of the mansion as quickly as I could. I couldn't help but think that if I had brought a camera, maybe I could have captured something here, just like at Bethany's Well.

Back in the lobby, I noticed a rack of brochures I had missed before. Flipping one open, I learned that the smaller Victorian home I had seen near the gate had originally been the Rosario Mansion. But after it was built, the Rosario family declared it not grand enough. They had gone on to construct this larger, more opulent home instead. The smaller house was eventually sold, and much of it had since been converted into apartments, helping the current owner maintain the estate.

I decided to check out the Tea Room Restaurant and see what snacks were available. If I ever made friends around here, it seemed like a nice place to have lunch. The best part was that you didn't need to pay admission for the house tour if you only went to the tea room—you just had to tell the cashier, then head upstairs by the gift shop.

I went up the stairs and entered the tea room. To my surprise, it was beautiful. The large space was arranged like a Victorian restaurant, complete with tea carts and fancy white lace tablecloths. Navy blue velvet drapes hung at the windows, tied back to reveal cream sheer curtains underneath. Dessert carts brimmed with cakes that looked absolutely decadent. The tea service cost around fifteen dollars and included tea sandwiches, hot tea, and a selection of old-fashioned cookies from the Victorian era, like ginger snaps.

The restaurant also had a menu with salads, sandwiches, and a few fried items such as chicken fingers. Nothing took long to prepare, and the prices were reasonable. The tea service was the only costly option.

I sat down at a window table, and a waitress came over with a menu. After looking it over, I decided on a slice of carrot cake and a pot of hot tea. The carrot cake was fantastic, and I knew I'd be back—if only for the Tea Room.

After finishing, I headed back to the hotel, unsure of what to do with the rest of the day. I figured I could rest and maybe grill a steak for a late lunch. Dinner at a restaurant was also an option, depending on how I felt later.

Back at the hotel, I noticed Jeanette's door open again as I walked past. Expecting her to have crew members inside, I glanced in, but she was alone, smoking in her smoke-free room. She had done the same in Miami, brushing off my concerns with the excuse that the company would cover any fines.

"Hey," Jeanette said as I passed.

I stopped at her door.

"Want to go with me to the courthouse?" she asked. "I'm looking into some property records. There's a burned foundation nearby—could've been a house or maybe a barn. If there's any record of it, it'll be at the courthouse."

Jeanette sighed and said, "You're probably doing something with Trevor anyway this weekend."

I let her believe it, even though I wasn't doing anything with him. For some reason, I felt she preferred the other crew's company to mine now. Maybe it was just me, but since her promotion to crew chief, I hadn't been as comfortable with her as a friend. Either way, I had a free weekend to myself.

"I hope you have a lovely afternoon," I told her. "I'll see you Monday at work."

Back in my room, I sat and thought for a while, flipping through the pictures I had taken at Bethany's Well. I reminded myself that I had research to do and a mystery to solve. Something was going on around this area—something I suspected was paranormal. I didn't believe in ghosts, but I couldn't deny feeling the presence of something evil at Bethany's Well, and that same sensation of being watched seemed to follow me throughout the town.

I read my Bible and prayed for about an hour. Afterward, I grilled a steak, baked a potato, and went for a swim. I spent the rest of the night watching a movie on TV. When I finally went to bed, I slept deeply and woke up feeling refreshed and relaxed for church the next morning.

I decided to save money by having breakfast at the hotel on Sunday morning, as I might want to eat out for lunch or dinner later. I made toast with peanut butter and had a glass of milk.

When I left for church, I arrived with plenty of time to spare and went inside. As I entered the sanctuary, I saw Lydia. She came over, said hello, and we chatted for a bit. I invited her to breakfast next Sunday morning, but she suggested lunch on Saturday instead.

"How about the Rosario Mansion's Tea Room Restaurant?" I asked.

"That sounds perfect," she said. "Let's meet at 12:30."

"Great. I'm looking forward to it," I replied.

I sat down in the back of the sanctuary, as I usually did, while she went up front to sit with her family. Lydia was married and had two young daughters.

After church, I decided to drive to a different town to get out for a while. Trevor still hadn't called or texted, so I tried calling him. My call went straight to voicemail. That had never happened before. I tried again, and the same thing happened. I suspected I might have been blocked, but it's also possible that his phone was off. I chose not to jump to conclusions just yet.

I drove for a while until I reached a town called Diamond Fields. There was a small mall there, along with several restaurants. I went inside the mall and wandered around, looking at the shops. Eventually, I stopped at the food court and ordered bourbon chicken with fried rice and vegetables, along with a Coke. I realized I hadn't eaten at a mall food court in years.

Afterward, I continued walking, thinking about buying gifts for family birthdays back home. The thought made me ache for Arizona. I missed my family and friends. I missed the deserts, historical sites, and natural wonders I had often visited, such as the Grand Canyon. More than anything, I missed home.

I shopped a little, then decided to head back to the hotel to swim and prepare for the coming week. As I was leaving the mall, I suddenly heard my name. It was the same female voice I had heard before at Bethany's Well. I froze and looked around, but no one was there. That was enough for me. I got into my car and drove straight back to the hotel.

The next morning, during the crew debriefing, we were told this would be our last week here. Some of us would be relocated to a new hotel to continue the pipeline project, while others would be reassigned. A few would be sent to the phase three excavation near the Rosario Mansion. Niles explained that if we were selected for phase three, he would hold a separate meeting later in the week.

I felt confident about my chances. I had been told during the hiring process that I might be considered for a phase three project down the line, and this seemed to be it. If chosen, I would get a new crew and a new crew chief. The thought brought me relief.

I also looked forward to my lunch with Lydia on Saturday. Things finally seemed to be turning in my favor.

For now, I focused on the week's work and prayed throughout the day, asking that, if it were God's will, I would be chosen for the transfer. I placed my trust in the Lord to guide me.

On Wednesday, while I was at work, I received a call from an Atlanta number—the area code for the company's office. I answered, and it was Cathy, the owner. She asked if I wanted to join the phase three project, and I gladly accepted without hesitation. Cathy explained that I would remain here for a few more weeks to help finish the pipeline survey with a handful of other crew members. After that, I would move into the Rosario House Apartments on a six-month lease while working on the excavation. Given my experience, she wanted me to be an integral part of the project. I thanked her and told her how excited I was to begin.

Relief washed over me. The thought of moving into such a beautiful place lifted my spirits, and I felt that God was working in my life. I continued to thank Him for this new opportunity.

That evening, I returned to the hotel feeling happy and rejuvenated. I spent time praying and reading the Bible. But still, I noticed Trevor hadn't reached out all week. I tried calling him, but only reached voicemail again.

The days passed quickly, and by Friday evening, many of the crew were preparing to relocate to their new assignments. Jeanette was one of them. As I walked past her open door, I saw her bed piled high with clothes as she packed. I kept moving toward my room, already thinking about the weekend.

I was looking forward to lunch with Lydia, but beyond that, I only had church planned. Maybe I will see a movie Saturday night. To celebrate the good news, I decided to go out to eat at Momma's Kitchen.

When I arrived in the town square, I spotted Trevor sitting in his car. He was on his cell phone, smiling, as though he was waiting for someone. Instead of stopping, I drove by and parked at Aurelio's Kitchen across the street so I could see who he was meeting.

About fifteen minutes later, a woman with straight brunette hair and brown eyes arrived. Trevor greeted her with a hug, and together they went into the bar.

I felt devastated. I wasn't sure why—after all, it had been clear he wasn't serious about me. Maybe it was just that he hadn't been honest. Instead of disappearing without a word, he could have told me he wasn't interested. That silence cut deeper than rejection ever would.

My heart began to pound, and anxiety surged through me as I helplessly watched Trevor and the woman walk into the bar, smiling and carefree. Embarrassment crept in at the thought of any of the crew seeing him with someone else. But most of them were leaving for another city far away, so that was unlikely. Still, I wished I hadn't seen it at all—that I had remained blissfully ignorant.

I drove on to Aurelio's Kitchen instead, not wanting to associate this memory with Momma's Kitchen. I ordered comfort food: a personal pepperoni pan pizza with a chocolate milkshake, and for dessert, a hot fudge brownie topped with vanilla ice cream. If nothing else, I could eat my feelings tonight.

Back at the hotel, I went for a swim. It was dark, but the pool lights glowed across the water, and I had the place to myself. Most of the crew were either out or packing. When I returned to my room, the sadness hit me harder than before. I prayed and read my Bible, but I couldn't focus. My thoughts kept drifting back to Trevor, and I knew I had to let him go.

Eventually, I lay down and tried to sleep, clinging to the thought that tomorrow would be better. I had lunch with Lydia, which gave me something to look forward to and hope. Still, I fell asleep feeling heavy with depression and sadness. Deep down, I knew it would get better—with time, and with God—but tonight, it didn't feel that way.

CHAPTER 6

$\mathcal{I}$ woke up early, dressed, and headed downstairs for breakfast at the hotel. A simple bowl of cereal and a glass of orange juice would be enough. I ate slowly, my eyes drifting toward the television mounted on the wall across from me. The morning news played, but my thoughts wandered elsewhere.

What could I do with myself until 12:30? Grocery shopping, maybe. I could fill the car with gas. Or perhaps I'd linger around the hotel for a while. There was no Trevor with whom to go out to dinner anymore. I tried to stay optimistic, reminding myself I still had church tomorrow, and maybe I'd check out the young adults' singles group the church offered.

After breakfast, I left the lobby and walked out to my car. I had no real destination, but at least a trip to the grocery store would pass the morning. I thought about the one near Momma's Kitchen. That store always had bright flowers outside and a bakery worth browsing.

When I arrived, the flowers were the first thing I noticed—rows of hanging baskets swaying gently in the breeze, rose bushes, and clusters of pink petunias. The sight stirred something in me, a stronger desire to have a garden of my own.

Inside, I passed the bakery. The warm aroma of apple pie spices filled the air, pulling me into a memory of my grandmother's kitchen. As a child, I always felt safe there, appreciated in a way I never did with my parents. They wanted me to play a role, to become someone plain and agreeable, someone who never asked for anything, never wanted anything—someone whose worth came only from serving others.

Maybe Trevor had brought that old ache to the surface. My parents had wanted a people-pleaser, not a person with her own thoughts and desires. I felt I had missed out on learning how to be myself, and instead had to stumble along, teaching myself lessons others my age already seemed to know.

I did the best I could, but sometimes it never felt like enough—for my parents, or for anyone else. That was how Trevor had treated me, too. I wasn't enough for him. I was supposed to fix his problems and somehow make everything wonderful. But why should I? He could do that for himself, just as my parents could.

I didn't care to be a people pleaser anymore, nor did I want to be the free therapist for friends and family. What mattered most were the two relationships I had to protect: how God felt about me, and how I felt about myself.

Right now, though, I was emotionally exhausted. The breakup with Trevor had left me raw and reflective, forcing me to face the patterns in my life that had led me here. Anger and rejection churned in me. Then, standing in the bakery aisle, it struck me—an epiphany. Trevor was of the world, and he wanted worldly things, not God. He hadn't been leading me closer to Him, but pulling me further away, trying to unravel my faith until I slipped back into the world I had left behind. He wasn't a blessing. He was a distraction, placed in my path by Satan to weaken my salvation.

But Satan would not win. I would not turn against God or stop following Him for the sake of Trevor. If anything, Satan had done me a favor by removing the very thing he had placed in my life to begin with. With that realization, I felt lighter. I finished my shopping, picking up a few steaks and more Coke. At least I could look forward to a week of good food.

Regret tugged at me for the comfort meal I had indulged in the night before, but it didn't matter now—I felt better. I prayed as I continued through the aisles, thanking God for opening my eyes to my past, for helping me understand why the breakup had happened, and for showing me how it was meant for my protection.

Back at the hotel, I put my groceries away and thought about how to pass the time until lunch. Downtown had antique shops and clothing stores, but I wasn't in the mood just yet. Instead, I decided to go for a walk to exercise. I remembered a small park near the town square and drove there, planning to walk a bit before meeting Lydia at the Tea Room.

Town Square Park was nestled between Momma's Kitchen and the town library. I pulled in and followed the winding cement path that curved beneath trees and past benches. A tennis court stood off to one side, and I wondered if someday I might meet someone there to play with.

The breeze picked up, rustling the leaves overhead, and the sunlight warmed my face as I walked. I prayed quietly as I went, reflecting on my hopes. I wanted a house of my own. I wanted to start a family. The fresh air, the exercise, and the prayers filled me with peace.

I sat on a bench for a while, watching a blue jay gather twigs and busy building its nest.

I glanced at my watch. It was 11:45 a.m. I headed toward my car, thinking that if I arrived early, I could spend more time browsing the gift shop. As I walked, a sudden burst of laughter drifted through the air. I stopped and looked around. No one was there. The voice was different from before, but the experience was the same. The laughter shifted into whispering, then back to laughter again, as if two people were carrying on a conversation just out of sight. The familiar sensation of being watched crept over me once more.

Then I heard the same female voice call my name. My heart raced. I walked faster toward my car, glancing over my shoulder with each step. Behind me, faint footsteps echoed. Panic hit. I broke into a run, yanked my door open, slammed it shut, and locked it. Trembling, I started the car and left the park, shaken.

As I drove, I prayed silently, asking God for help and for the truth to be revealed. I stopped at the grocery store I had been at earlier and parked. Getting out, I went to the Coke machine out front, bought a can of soda, and drank it in my car, hoping it would steady my nerves. Slowly, my heartbeat calmed, and the shaking eased.

Feeling a little better, I drove off to Rosario Mansion to meet Lydia for lunch, arriving in about twenty minutes. With extra time to spare, I wandered through the gift shop again, this time studying the clothes and shoes. A pair of silver heels with intricate beadwork caught my eye—perfect for the flapper dress for sale nearby.

When I looked up, Lydia was standing there, smiling. For a moment, I had forgotten about her while shopping. "What do you think about these shoes?" I asked, holding them up.

"I like them," she said warmly.

I smiled. "Maybe I'll get them after lunch."

We headed upstairs to the restaurant. A hostess greeted us and led us to a table by the window.

"Do you want to try the tea time experience?" I asked Lydia as she opened her menu.

She shook her head slightly. "I think I'm more in the mood for a salad—and maybe a piece of chocolate cake."

I decided on the tea time experience for myself. "I'll see what's included, and if I'm still hungry afterward, I'll order something else."

I chose cinnamon tea and Earl Grey. The waitress returned with a polished silver kettle filled with hot water, a selection of old-fashioned cookies—ginger snaps and sugar cookies—and a small holder filled with more tea options. She placed the tea sandwiches in front of me: dozens of little crustless triangles filled with different meats and spreads. Although there was more food than I expected, the tea time experience turned out to be delightful.

Lydia was quiet at first, but as lunch went on, she grew more talkative and began to open up. I told her about Trevor and how uncertain things felt right now—how it was an exciting but difficult time because only God knows what He might bring into my life, or who. Lydia spoke about her job and her family. She seemed genuinely happy and was clearly a devoted Christian. I felt I could learn a lot from her.

I didn't tell her yet about my own longing for a home and family. The situation with Trevor had been hard on my heart, and even bringing it up embarrassed me. I wanted to move on.

Lydia talked about her husband, who sounded like a kind man. He helped out at home because she worked too. The conversation shifted to local activities, as I'd be staying longer with the phase three project approaching. She mentioned a city about an hour and a half away with a mall, great shopping, plenty of restaurants, and a movie theater.

"Would you want to go there with me sometime?" I asked.

"I'd love to," she said with a smile. "We could shop and see a movie soon."

"Perfect," I replied. "I'll look forward to it."

We said our goodbyes, promising to see each other at church tomorrow. As she walked away, I felt a pang of sadness. Being alone again hit me harder than usual, especially with the breakup with Trevor and the strange, unsettling experiences around town.

Back at the hotel, I wondered what to do with the rest of my day. A movie sounded fun. I hadn't been in a long time, and the thought of buttery popcorn made me smile. For now, though, I stayed in my room, rested, and watched TV for a while. I prayed and read my Bible afterward, but Trevor still crept into my thoughts from time to time. I wished it would stop.

I had passed a local movie theater before and had a good idea of when movies started on Saturdays. I called the theater to check what was playing and at what times. Deciding on a comedy about a fumbled bank robbery set in the Old West, I planned to head out soon to watch it.

I left my room and headed to my car. At the picnic area, Niles and a few of his crew friends were grilling steaks and hamburgers. Niles spotted me, called out a hello, and asked if I wanted to join them at the pool later.

"Thanks, but I'm going to a movie," I told him. "I won't be back until much later."

He didn't seem happy with my answer. In fact, he looked annoyed, as though I'd snubbed them by not coming over. They had never paid me much attention before, and I wasn't about to change my plans just because he wanted me to.

I left and went to the movie. It was good, and I treated myself to popcorn and a large Coke. It felt nice to get out, even if I was by myself. Still, I told myself the next movie I went to see would be with someone special.

The next morning, I went to church. After the sermon, I joined the Bible study group for young adult singles. The room was full of people my age. Most of them seemed indifferent to me, but I made an effort to talk and introduce myself. I wasn't sure if I would find love in this group, but I hoped to make some friends at least, given that I would be here for at least another six months.

Even so, my primary focus was on learning more about the Bible and growing closer to God. Within the larger group, I formed a connection with a smaller circle: a kind young woman named Mary and her two friends, Matthew and Luke. They were among the few who seemed genuinely interested in speaking with me.

Still, I couldn't shake the feeling that I didn't belong. I prayed about it, and the thought that came to me was, *It's your clothes. They don't think you have nice clothes.* That stung. Most of what I wore came from clearance racks at Macy's. I hadn't grown up with much, and my style reflected that—serviceable, affordable, but not fashionable. The thought left me feeling a little depressed as I left the group. I decided I would return a few more times before making up my mind.

On my way out, I ran into Lydia. She explained she had been running late and hadn't made it to the Bible study. Instead, she went straight to the service, but because the sanctuary was full, she sat in the overflow area. The church converted a former banquet hall into a large room equipped with TV screens, allowing members to watch the sermon while making more seats available for visitors.

"Hi, I'm glad you stopped to talk," I told Lydia.

She smiled warmly. "So, how was the young adults group?"

"I went," I said. "I'll see how it goes in the future, but I'm not sure it's the right Bible study for me."

"You could always join my group instead. It's more of a general Bible study."

"I'll consider it."

Just then, her daughters ran up to her, followed closely by her husband. I could tell she was busy, so I said, "I'll see you soon. Have a good day."

"Goodbye," she said, still smiling. "I hope to see you again soon."

After we parted ways, I wasn't sure what to do with the rest of my Sunday off. I took a long drive, lost in thought and prayer. When I returned to town, I stopped for lunch at Momma's Kitchen. It turned out to be a mistake—the place was crowded with families fresh from church. I sat at the coffee counter, like I had the first time I ate there.

A waitress handed me a menu. "What can I get you today?"

"Spaghetti, please," I said, surprising even myself. It felt like an odd choice, especially since Aurelio's Restaurant was better known for spaghetti. Still, it turned out to be good, and the breadsticks were excellent—a pleasant surprise.

Afterward, I thought about walking around the town square to window shop, to get out for the day before heading back to the hotel. That was when my cell phone rang. The number was Jeanette's.

"Hey," I answered. "How are you doing?"

"I'm good," she said. She told me about her new project and how glad she was to be away from Niles.

I mentioned, almost without thinking, "He asked me to come to the pool the other night."

Her tone shifted instantly, sharp and annoyed. "He only said that because no one else was at the hotel. You know that."

The way she said it felt mean and cold. I hadn't thought it was a big deal, but I could tell she was implying I must like Niles. I didn't. I had no feelings for him, and I didn't care to be caught up in the feud she had with him and his friends on the crew.

After the call ended, I had a feeling I probably wouldn't hear from Jeanette again. Oddly enough, I didn't mind. It seemed increasingly that she thrived on drama and gossip. I wanted friends who were positive and supportive—people who lifted others, not tore them down.

Jeanette went on about her project as I listened. She was hoping to be promoted within the company. I told her I hoped she would and wished her the best. Still, I had a feeling that drama was already brewing on her new project. I hoped I was wrong, but at least she seemed to be enjoying the work. After a while, we hung up, and it felt as though I had lost my old friend.

I was starting to realize it was okay to move on—to let people be, even if that meant they no longer wanted a friendship with me. I also came to realize that the world would reject me, regardless of my actions or words. Why should I try to get along with people who only cared about how I could benefit them? God's love wasn't like that. He loved me regardless of what I could or couldn't do for Him.

The next morning, I got up and went to work as usual. The crew was only a fraction of what it used to be, but I liked it better that way. The tension between Jeanette and Niles was gone, and the atmosphere had shifted. Most of the crew now were Niles's friends, and though I had been wary at first, they were cordial. I appreciated working alongside them to help finish the project.

There were a lot of good things about Niles's friends—things I was afraid Jeanette had never wanted to see. She had let her offense define everyone connected to him. At least it was quiet now, and I welcomed the silence and peace I was beginning to experience.

CHAPTER 7

*R*osario House, 1970

Brenda and Debra sat in the dining room, playing with a few board games they had found around the house. One of them stood out—an odd-looking game neither of their parents had purchased. They had no idea how it had gotten there, but it looked intriguing.

The game was called *Ouija Board*. The girls read the instructions and set it up. Brenda, the oldest at ten, went first. Debra, only seven, watched closely. Brenda held the cursor over the letters, her long golden hair falling in her face as she leaned over the dining table.

Slowly, the letters began to form words. Then, words became sentences. Brenda tried to hold the cursor steady, but it seemed to move on its own. The first sentence appeared: *Under the blood, I hate you. Leave now.*

The same sentence repeated three times.

Debra leaned forward. "Let me try. Maybe I can make it say something more interesting."

Reluctantly, Brenda handed her the cursor. Debra placed her hands on it, and again the letters began to move: *Under the blood, I hate you. Get out now.* Three times in a row.

"Stop making it say that," Brenda snapped.

"I'm not!" Debra shot back, staring at her sister. "I thought *you* were the one doing it. I thought you were trying to scare me."

Both girls went silent, realizing the truth. Neither of them had moved the cursor. The sentences had spelled themselves. Then, just as they pushed the game aside, the board flew off the table and slammed against the wall eight feet away.

Debra's eyes widened. "This reminds me of a dream I had," she whispered. "In my dream, people carried black mirrors. They used them to talk to each other all over the world. The mirrors knew where people were, and you could speak into them and someone far away would hear you."

Brenda shivered. The dream felt like a premonition, and so did the words on the board. She understood the phrase *under the blood*—a reference to salvation. Their family was Christian, and they had only recently moved into the house. It wasn't a mansion like the grand estate across the way, but it was large, and the family was grateful to have it.

Debra lowered her voice. "I've seen the Grey Lady, too."

Brenda frowned. "Who's the Grey Lady? Where did you see her?"

Debra's gaze was steady, unblinking. "Sometimes she floats above your bed, watching you. She's dressed in all grey, and even her skin is grey. But I can't see her face. She wears a veil, and it spreads out like it's floating in water—like it's moving in the wind—while she hangs above us in the dark."

Debra's voice dropped to a whisper. "The Lady in Grey... she's around the bad guy, too."

Brenda stared at her sister. "What bad guy?" she asked in disbelief.

"The laughing man," Debra replied. "He comes looking for the people he's been assigned to harm. He thinks destroying them is funny, even entertaining. The more damage he causes, the more amusing it becomes to him and his friend. He's not a good person."

Brenda's face went pale. She had heard faint laughing around the house, too—sometimes at night, sometimes when she was alone. And a few times, a woman's voice had called her name when no one was there.

She swallowed hard, trying not to show her fear. She could sometimes feel the presence of something watching her, a heavy sense of being observed. She knew it wasn't good. Whatever it was, it seemed to want to harm the family if it could.

Brenda also knew why they could afford the mansion. It had been on the market for years, but it was impossible to sell because of the town's history and its association with Bethany's Well. The city had nearly emptied after a terrible incident long ago—a woman had sought revenge on the cruel town by poisoning its once-healthy water. Since then, the place had become infamous for strange occurrences and paranormal events tied to that tragedy.

Rosario House, 2006

I heard from Cathy by email on Monday—she told me I would be moving into my studio apartment at Rosario House Apartments next Friday. She gave me the weekend to move everything out of the hotel and settle into the apartment.

I was excited to finally have a place of my own. I couldn't wait to see what it looked like. From Cathy's description, it was partially furnished and already had some essentials: pots, pans, silverware, a toaster, and a microwave. I would still need to pick up a tea kettle and a few other things, but the basics were covered.

Even if it was only for six months, having my own place felt like a step in the right direction. It would give me stability and a chance to attend church regularly. I couldn't wait to go shopping and pick out things for the apartment, though I decided to wait until I saw what was already there.

The two weeks passed quickly. By Friday evening, I pulled into the Rosario House Apartments. The building was off-white, matching the Rosario Mansion across the street. I parked in the small lot out front. Most of the apartments were located on the left side of the house, while the owners still lived on the right. In the middle of the home was the office and a small lobby where residents could use the free Wi-Fi, relax on comfortable couches, or watch TV. There was a drink station with coffee and tea, and often snacks—cookies and muffins. Across from the TV were two business desks equipped with computers and a printer for tenants' use.

The house was old but well cared for. I went to the office and knocked on the door. A middle-aged woman answered. She introduced herself as Brenda and explained that she and her younger sister, Debra, owned the property.

"We inherited the house from our parents," she said.

"I'm sorry to hear they've passed," I replied gently.

Brenda shook her head. "Oh, no, they're alive and well. They no longer wanted to manage the apartments. They're enjoying retirement now."

I smiled, relieved.

She walked me to my unit, explaining along the way that the apartments didn't have individual washers or dryers, but there was a laundry room with two of each, free to use. Tenants just needed to provide their own soap and supplies.

As we reached my door, she added, "This unit has a dishwasher and a lovely bay window. The house is old—it's easier to have a shared laundry room than to run new pipes through a building like this. There are fourteen units total, all studios, and it's a two-story home."

I nodded, eager to step inside and see my new space.

As we walked to the unit, I realized it was on the first floor. I thought that was a good thing—no climbing stairs every day, especially since the old house didn't have an elevator. Still, I hoped the neighbors upstairs would be quiet.

When we arrived, Brenda unlocked the door and pushed it open. I stepped back, caught off guard. I hadn't expected the apartment to be so pretty. It wasn't fancy or overly decorated, but elegant and simple. Oak floors stretched across the room, and the off-white walls gave it a clean, calm feel. A lovely bay window stood out, framed by sheer off-white curtains beneath heavier off-white drapes. Two plant shelves were built into the window frame, and I immediately imagined buying plants to put there.

To the left was a kitchenette with oak cabinets, a white electric stove, a white dishwasher, and a white refrigerator. To the right sat a full-size bed with a single wooden nightstand painted dark blue, topped with a gold metal lamp. A small dresser, painted to match, stood nearby, with a TV mounted above it instead of a mirror.

In the center of the room, a light blue kitchen table with four chairs matched the space. Under the bay window, a small light blue couch sat across from an oak coffee table, flanked by two accent chairs upholstered in blue with white floral designs.

The apartment had far more furniture than I expected, especially for a place described as "partially furnished." I even noticed a microwave above the stove—one less thing I'd need to buy.

Brenda pointed toward the back wall. "The restroom's over there. There should be a few towels and other basics. There's also a small walk-in closet, but no hangers—you'll need to pick some up. And the drawers should already have a set of silverware."

"Thank you for showing me around," I said. "I think I'll head out now to grab some food and pick up a few household things I'll need."

She handed me the key. "Here you go."

I stepped into the hallway, grateful and excited. I liked Brenda and hoped she might be someone I could talk to occasionally at the complex. Still, there was something in her demeanor—a hint of unease. I got the feeling she didn't really like living here, though I couldn't yet guess why.

At the grocery store, I picked up a few items I could find there before heading to a larger store with a housewares department. I brought the bags back to the apartment, then returned to the hotel for my last night. I planned to finish packing, load the car in the morning, and say farewell to the place. I knew I would miss the complimentary breakfast every morning, as well as the pool.

I decided to squeeze in one last swim before leaving, so I went for a dip as soon as I got back. The rest of the crew would be checking out tomorrow, too, heading to their new hotels for new projects. I didn't know much about where most of them were going; they hadn't said.

After getting out of the pool, I returned to my hotel room and started packing. The swim had left me refreshed, and I reached for a Coke in the mini refrigerator when my cell phone rang. I glanced at the caller ID and recognized the number.

"Hello?" I answered.

It was Jenny. She asked how I was doing, and I told her about finishing the phase three project and moving into an apartment for the next six months.

"I'm working on another pipeline survey down in Texas," she said. "Jeanette's on the same project with me."

That surprised me. "How's she doing?" I asked.

"She's alright," Jenny said after a pause. "She... mentioned you. She told me you liked Niles."

I froze. "What do you mean by that?"

Jenny hesitated, then added, "She seemed to mean it… romantically."

I thought about it for a moment before answering. "Maybe it could be perceived that Jeanette and I had a falling out, but that's all. I don't think we're friends anymore. If I ran into her on another project, she'd be a former coworker I knew."

I made my point clear. "It has nothing to do with Niles. I don't like him romantically. The truth is that Jeanette acted inappropriately and unprofessionally at times when she was crew chief, and that put distance between us. On top of that, I didn't want to get dragged into her grudge against Niles."

Jenny didn't respond much after that. She ended the call quickly, and I got the impression the only reason she had called was to carry this conversation back to others later.

Still, the call confirmed what I had already suspected: Jeanette wasn't a friend. She had been gossiping about me to coworkers, spinning some story about fictitious feelings for Niles, trying to blame that for the rift between us.

I considered calling Jeanette to clear things up, but that would mean telling her that Jenny had shared her thoughts with me. I had already explained my side, and it may be best to let it drop. Hopefully, I'd never hear about the topic again. I couldn't help but feel that Jenny wasn't much of a friend either—just someone who wanted something to talk about.

After the call ended, I felt hurt and disappointed. At one time, I had really liked both Jeanette and Jenny. But moments like this served as reminders to be mindful of what I shared with people. It takes time to learn someone's true character. Those who push you to share personal information quickly rarely have good intentions for wanting to know so much about you so soon.

Exhausted, I went to sleep not long after the call so I could get up early, pack, and move out in the morning.

The alarm went off at 8:00 AM. I still felt tired, but I reminded myself I could always take a nap that afternoon. I hauled my two suitcases to the car, along with a few garbage bags filled with odds and ends—like my CD player and other things I didn't want taking up space in my luggage. It took about thirty minutes to load everything.

Afterward, I went to the lobby for my last complimentary breakfast.

Peanut butter on toast, a bowl of cereal, and orange juice—my usual. Then I went to the front desk, checked out, and headed to the car.

Driving away, I felt sad. Sad for everything that had happened at that hotel—Trevor, Jeanette, all of it.

But when I arrived at my new apartment, the sadness lifted. It felt good to finally have a home. I carried my luggage inside, grateful I had bought hangers at the store the night before. They weren't the best quality, but they would do. I hadn't wanted to spend much on them anyway—not when I might move out in six months and end up discarding them before going back to hotel living.

I decided to leave my luggage for later and started setting up the kitchen first. Cooking for myself again was what I was most excited about. I opened the refrigerator door and smiled. A full-size fridge at last. It felt like freedom after months of living with hotel mini-fridges.

The unit had pots, pans, and a few frying pans. I rummaged through everything to see what I had and what I would need. I was pleased to discover a few kitchen utensils, including spatulas, a ladle, and several large serving spoons. Even better, tucked away in the cabinet was an old crock-pot. Life was looking up, and I paused to pray and thank God for His blessings.

I had enough to get by for now, so I didn't need to buy anything else. I was still glad I had purchased the hangers last night, though. With that in mind, I focused on unpacking my luggage into the closet and dresser. Miscellaneous items went into the two bottom drawers, while my socks and undergarments filled the smaller ones. I hung up my clothes in the closet, grateful to see everything finally in order.

Unpacking took me about three hours, possibly a bit longer. When I finished, I decided to treat myself to lunch at Momma's Kitchen, then pick up groceries while I was in town. As I walked down the hallway toward the parking lot, my next-door neighbor to the right greeted me with a quiet "Hi."

"Hi," I replied, smiling as I turned the corner. For some reason, I couldn't help but notice that he was still watching me. I caught myself smiling at his slight interest.

At Momma's Kitchen, I ordered a steak with a baked potato and was seated in the main dining room near the fireplace. The atmosphere was pleasant, and I appreciated the cool air inside after spending the morning unpacking and setting up the apartment.

When I got home, I rested, watched some TV, read the Bible, and prayed. I went to bed early, and I slept well. In the morning, I got up, dressed for church, and fixed my first meal in the new kitchen: eggs, toast, and a tall glass of orange juice.

At church, I attended the adult singles class again. Luke was there, talking with Mary and Matthew, but I noticed he glanced at me now and then, picking up on small details. He seemed sweet, and regardless of anything else, I thought he would make a lovely friend. I liked that he was half Italian—Italy had always fascinated me. Taking Latin in high school had sparked my interest in antiquity and archaeology, and the thought of Italian culture and history had stayed with me ever since.

I asked Luke if he had ever been to Italy. He smiled and said he hadn't, but he hoped to go someday soon. I told him I hoped so for him, too. I could imagine he must have grown up with excellent meals, given his mother's Italian heritage.

I left the church feeling better, as if I was starting to connect with people. On my way out, I ran into Lydia again. She was busy with her family, but she stopped long enough to ask, "Would you like to come to a ladies' event next Saturday? We'll have a guest speaker, and lunch will be served. It starts at ten and goes until noon, then lunch afterward."

"Thank you," I said. "I'll be there."

She smiled warmly, and I waved goodbye. "See you later," I told her, already looking forward to it.

CHAPTER 8

I went to bed excited for my first day of work tomorrow on my new phase three project. After reading the Bible and praying, I got ready for bed. It felt good to meal prep for tomorrow in my own apartment. I lay down and tried to fall asleep, but for some reason, my mind was full of thoughts.

Eventually, I drifted off, and Bethany appeared in my dream again. She was standing just outside the schoolhouse with the friend she had been speaking to in the first dream.

The friend turned to her. "Jocelyn came to talk to me about you a month or so ago. She told me you were talking about her in class that day."

Bethany looked surprised.

"I told Jocelyn that neither of us mentioned her at all in our conversations," the friend went on. "I defended you. But she didn't believe me. She even called you names that no respectable lady should call another."

The friend shook her head. "It's not worth talking to Jocelyn about it. She's popular, and it's gone to her head—being wealthy and well-liked in this small town. I don't think she's right, but she won't listen to reason. She's already made up her mind to get revenge over something that never even happened."

Bethany lowered her gaze. She had noticed that whenever Jocelyn was around, she would give her hateful looks and whisper about her to friends, saying she thought too much of herself, calling her ugly and a bad person. Bethany tried to ignore everything, focusing on completing her final year of school so she could move on to high school.

I woke up unsettled, wondering why I kept having these dreams of Bethany. I sympathized with her, but was it real? Had any of this actually happened? Bethany's Well turned out not to exist—or at least, I thought it didn't. I had seen something. But now I was starting to feel that a demonic entity might be trying to tell me something...or trying to trick me. I didn't know yet what Bethany's story really meant.

I got ready for work and drove my own car to the project site. I did miss using company vehicles to get to project sites, though. The site was, ironically, close to Bethany's Well—right off the same side road. Instead of turning right toward the Well, I had driven straight a short distance farther, and there it was, off to the left, surrounded by woods. I hadn't realized how close I was to my future phase three project.

I parked my car and walked up to the excavation site, taking a moment to survey it. The units were already set up or marked off with string, dividing them into neat 2x2-meter squares. They were all under a tent, which made me smile. Having shade in the summer was a blessing. Although it didn't always happen, it made the work much easier when it did.

The crew chief came over and introduced himself as Derek. He showed me around the site and assigned me to a unit. I had my gear in my backpack, along with some borrowed company equipment, so I set up and got to work. Before long, two coworkers began working in the units beside mine. One of them reached out to shake my hand.

"I'm Jasper," he said, taking the unit on my right.

The other, a much younger guy, introduced himself as Edward. He had just graduated from college, and this was his first project. He took the unit to my left.

Edward was excited about the opportunity, and both he and Jasper were cheerful and easy to talk to. Time passed quickly, and before I realized it, another new coworker appeared on the other side of Jasper. She smiled at me warmly, and right before lunch, she came over.

"I'm Christine," she said, her tone friendly.

So far, I've liked everyone I've met, but I still carry the sting of rejection from what happened with Trevor. I didn't want to sit alone, so when Jasper invited me to join him and his group for lunch, I accepted. I could use a friend or two.

He was sitting with the crew he called his own: Alma, an older woman, and two younger guys named Antonio and Marshall. Antonio and Marshall were cold and distant toward me, but Jasper and Alma were friendly, with Jasper usually leading the conversation and Alma chiming in as the runner-up.

The group felt a little uneasy due to the tension Antonio and Marshall gave off, but I let it go. I ate my lunch quietly and joined in the conversation here and there. Afterward, I went back to work, losing track of time again until Derek came over and reminded me I had less than thirty minutes to wrap up. We would need to cover the units with tarps before the end of the day.

AT THE END of the day, I went back to my new apartment feeling accomplished. I got cleaned up, grateful that I wasn't as filthy as I used to be after working in the deep woods, hacking my way through thorny plants just to do a shovel test. The best part was that Jeanette wasn't involved in this project. I felt a growing sense of relief at having work that gave me peace.

For dinner, I made meatloaf and mashed potatoes. Cooking in my own kitchen thrilled me, but as I sat down to eat, I realized I was eating alone again. I hadn't felt that kind of loneliness in a while. It came and went, lingering in the background of my life—especially since the breakup with Trevor. I didn't want to be alone anymore.

I spent the evening watching TV, then went to bed after my Bible study and prayers. When I woke up, I didn't feel very rested, but I still looked forward to work. At the site, I greeted Jasper and Edward and waved to Christine from a distance. Jasper was his usual self—talking to everyone and cracking jokes as he worked. I found myself drawn to the noise and chatter. He was filling a void in my life. Silence was what I couldn't stand right now.

When lunch approached, I sat with Jasper and his crew again. We talked about nothing in particular, but it was comforting. Alma began opening up a little more, sharing details about her life. I felt as though I belonged—not as a close friend, but at least as part of the group. A here-today, gone-tomorrow coworker. And that was enough for me.

This continued all week until Saturday. I was getting ready to attend the church function Lydia had invited me to. I dressed up a little, but not much —just a long floral skirt with a matching top and a pair of sandals. It looked nice, but felt like a low-effort Saturday morning.

As I was leaving for church, a necklace on my dresser suddenly fell to the floor. It hadn't been near the edge, and with no one else in the apartment, I had no idea how it had happened. I looked around suspiciously, hoping there wasn't any paranormal activity here. I prayed for God to remove any spirit that wasn't the Holy Ghost.

At the church, I found Lydia, who sat beside me. The event was held in the banquet room, where numerous white folding tables were covered with floral tablecloths. A buffet line was set up at the front, still empty for the moment. Mary from the young adults' singles class waved at me. I waved back, and she came over to sit beside me. As we talked, I learned that Mary was going through a bad breakup, just like me.

We didn't discuss it much at the event, but I felt it could help us bond and develop a sense of camaraderie. The gathering was pleasant, and the guest speaker encouraged us to draw closer to God and trust Him to guide our lives. Afterward, we were served salad, broccoli cheese soup, and assorted sandwiches with individual bags of potato chips. Drinks included soda, sweet tea, and unsweetened tea.

I stayed until the event ended and the church members began cleaning up. I could have paid a little more attention to Lydia while Mary was there, but Lydia was popular in the church and had many people wanting to talk with her as they passed by. I doubted I would have gotten much attention from her anyway.

After the church event, I went back home and passed my neighbor, who noticed I was dressed nicely. He smiled and greeted me as we crossed paths, then stopped, turned around, and introduced himself as Thomas. He made small talk and asked where I had gone on a Saturday morning, dressed up. I told him about the church event, and soon we were discussing our jobs and sharing a bit about our lives. Eventually, he said he had to get to work. He was a contractor working in the area for a while, much like me. When I finally stepped inside my apartment, I realized we had been standing in the hallway talking for an hour.

I wasn't sure how to spend my weekends anymore with the new kitchen, as I used to enjoy going out to eat. I decided to start looking for more historical places to visit, as well as parks and natural attractions. I was also considering planning a long weekend trip to the mountains. I had been wanting a vacation for quite some time.

What I liked most about my apartment was the quietness of the neighbors above me. It gave me a peaceful place to live. My life was good in that moment, and I was thankful to God for it. I decided to go out for a vanilla chai tea at Momma's Kitchen.

I sat at the coffee counter and ordered a brownie to go along with my tea. I lingered there for a while, watching out the window and letting my mind wander. I told myself that next weekend would be better, as I would find something entertaining to do.

Sunday morning, I went to church, then returned to the apartment to rest and make myself a nice lunch. On a whim, I made breakfast for lunch: pancakes with maple syrup, scrambled eggs, sausage patties, and bacon, topped off with a glass of orange juice.

After cleaning up, most of the afternoon had slipped away. I sat down to write for a while. I had been working on a novel I wanted to finish, but traveling so much for work had slowed progress. Before bed, I prayed and read the Bible, then turned in early to prepare for Monday morning.

I arrived at work on Monday, looking forward to the day and to talking with my coworkers. The hours passed as usual, but I noticed Alma came up to me and made small talk. She seemed to be opening up. The day ended, and as the week went on, things continued much the same.

After a few weeks, we had all gotten acquainted, and I felt happy to be part of this project. Alma had become friendly, often talking about her family and hobbies. Jasper never discussed personal matters, but he was pleasant and kept conversations lighthearted.

One afternoon, when I returned from work, I saw Brenda in the lobby and asked how she was doing. She smiled and said she was fine, then asked how I liked living in the apartment complex.

"It's nice," I told her. "I like it."

She didn't seem convinced. Her expression shifted, almost unimpressed. "Why don't you believe me?" I asked.

Brenda sighed and looked down. My suspicion grew; she clearly knew something about the place that she wasn't sharing. Why had she even brought it up?

"When you start to experience strange things around the apartment," she said at last, her tone heavy, "then we'll talk."

I studied her face. "Does this have anything to do with the paranormal activity people claim happens around here?"

Brenda's expression hardened. With a serious, almost fearful look, she said quietly, "Unfortunately, you may find out."

My chest tightened. "Does this have to do with Bethany's Well specifically?"

She nodded once. "That incident was one of his handiworks." Without another word, she turned and walked away.

I stood there, confused and unsettled. Who was she talking about? And how could it have been someone's handiwork from 1890?

I went back to my apartment and passed by Thomas again. He waved and asked how I was doing.

"Pretty good," I said, then lowered my voice. "Have you ever experienced anything odd around this apartment complex?"

He shrugged. "A few things. But I work so much, I'm hardly ever home to notice anything."

"Why do you ask?" he added.

"I just heard the place is… more or less haunted."

Thomas gave me an odd look, then smirked. "I'd believe it."

"That's not exactly reassuring," I replied.

He laughed. "If you get scared, call me. I'll come over and chase the ghost off for you."

I smiled. "It's a deal."

He headed off toward the grocery store while I returned to my apartment.

On Sunday, I attended the young single adult group again, though I still felt unsure about it. I liked Mary and the twins, but the rest of the group didn't seem overly interested in me. During the meeting, Mary suggested we all meet at a restaurant next Saturday night. I agreed, thinking it might be fun. I noticed Luke watching me more closely than the others, almost eager for my response when I said yes.

For the rest of Sunday, I spent time at home writing. I made a cup of tea and sat on the couch by my bay window, enjoying the lovely day as warm sunlight spilled into the room.

Monday morning, I went to work and noticed Jasper wasn't there. Derek mentioned he had called off. I focused a little more on talking to Edward, who worked in the unit to my left. He also liked to write, so I shared some of my storyline ideas to hear his thoughts. He had plenty of good suggestions, and I hoped we would stay in touch after the project. He mentioned he was also trying to build a successful channel on a new video-sharing website called YouTube. I had never heard of it before, but he said it had just been released this year.

At lunch, I sat with Jasper's crew again. Alma talked to me, but she seemed a little grumpy. I assumed it had something to do with her personal life and left it at that. I tried to cheer her up, staying positive, but I think she may have taken it as if I were being slightly condescending.

I worked through the rest of the day, losing track of time after lunch as the hours slipped by. When the day ended, I packed up, pulled the tarp over my unit, and weighed the sides down with rocks to keep it steady in the wind. Then I headed home.

Dinner that night was steak and mashed potatoes. I wasn't sure why I felt like treating myself, but maybe it was because I was still feeling a little down about Trevor. The pain had eased over time, and I didn't think of him as often anymore, but when I did, it still hurt.

After eating, I read the Bible and prayed for a while before deciding to go to bed early and try to get some sleep. As I lay there, I thought about how nice it had been having quiet neighbors upstairs and how comfortable the apartment felt. I hoped it would stay that way—and that I would never discover what Brenda meant when she warned me that "someone is here."

The next morning, I woke up drained, not as rested as I had hoped to be for another long day at work. Still, I got ready and went in. Jasper was back that day, and I felt a little lighter just having him around to crack jokes.

CHAPTER 9

$\mathcal{I}$ began to wonder who Brenda meant by "someone" in the context of the apartment. Lost in thought about it, I had completely forgotten Jasper was there today. He seemed to notice but said nothing, continuing to work quietly on excavating his unit.

When lunch came, I noticed Alma was still off and unusually quiet. I didn't talk much either, drifting in and out of my own thoughts as the conversation around me blurred into background noise. A strange feeling crept over me—I felt watched. I glanced around, but no one was looking at me. The feeling only grew stronger as the day went on, as if something was out there. Watching. Waiting. For what, I didn't know, and I didn't want to find out.

As I cleaned up for the day, a faint laughter floated from the woods. My heart skipped. Somehow, I knew he was here. I didn't know who yet, but I knew it wasn't good.

I went home, hoping to relax and forget about work. Things seemed better once I walked inside. I put a frozen lasagna dish in the oven, planning to stretch the family-size portion over three nights. I preferred eating most of my meals in the evening to avoid going to bed hungry.

While the food baked, I read the Bible and prayed. I asked God to remove any spirit there that wasn't the Holy Ghost. Slowly, the presence I'd felt earlier began to fade, and for the first time all day, I felt alone in my apartment. I kept praying until dinner was ready, then ate in silence. The loneliness weighed on me. For a moment, I even considered going to Momma's Kitchen to get a tea and be around people.

Then I sensed it again—the presence. It had moved. It was now in the apartment above me. Strangely, I felt a mix of relief and dread as I prepared for bed, hoping for sleep.

I tried to fall asleep but couldn't. I lay there in the dark until I finally drifted off—only to be jolted awake by a loud thud above me. Something heavy, but not large, had been dropped, the noise sharp and concentrated.

It struck me as odd. I had never heard a sound from the neighbors before. Rolling over, I tried to go back to sleep.

When my alarm went off in the morning, I felt unrested, my head thick with exhaustion. I considered calling out of work but decided to go anyway, telling myself I'd stick to low, easy tasks for the day.

I made breakfast and decided on cereal that morning; I didn't feel like cooking, and I needed to make up for the time I'd lost sleeping in. Sitting at the table, staring blankly at my bowl, I heard stomping above me. This time it felt deliberate. I had never heard anything like it before, and I'd lived there long enough to know I had quiet neighbors. Maybe they'd moved out and someone new had moved in. I told myself I'd ask Brenda about it the next time I saw her.

At work, I tried to take my mind off the apartment, letting Jasper lighten the mood and make me laugh. That morning, I worked on paperwork and assisted with tasks outside my unit, including reviewing photograph logs and helping with the inventory of artifacts to be sent to the laboratory.

By lunchtime, I felt better and more awake, ready to return to my unit. But as I settled back into the rhythm of work, something occurred to me— something I hadn't noticed before, probably because I'd been too tired. Jasper wasn't really funny to most people. His jokes barely landed with the crew. It seemed I was the only one who shared his sense of humor.

I didn't know how to take that. It felt uncomfortably familiar. My first dream had been to become a comedian, but even then, I'd been the only one who found myself funny. Had I been blind to Jasper's lame jokes this whole time? And what did that say about my own sense of humor?

As I drifted into an existential crisis, I glanced around and saw the hidden eye rolls and half-hearted laughs as Jasper moved from person to person, talking. The crew liked him—he was well treated—but I finally saw that, in their eyes, he wasn't hilarious.

Thankfully, the day came to an end. I went home, heated up leftover lasagna in the microwave, and tried to watch TV while I ate dinner. Above me, the apartment's TV blared loudly—a sound I had never heard before—as heavy footsteps echoed on the ceiling.

After dinner, I decided to take a drive to the drugstore where I'd had my film developed. I wandered through the aisles, casually shopping but secretly on a mission to find earplugs. They would come in handy if the noise continued above me tonight.

As I rounded the corner of an aisle, I ran into Trevor by accident. He didn't see me, and I quickly turned away, ducking into the next aisle. I waited a few minutes, listening as he spoke on his cell phone about his plans for the evening—a meeting at a bowling alley. I loved bowling, and the thought sparked an idea. Maybe I'd ask Mary and the twins if they wanted to go soon.

I could still hear Trevor talking, so I waited until he had left. Then I wandered the aisles, pretending to shop until he checked out. Only after he was gone did I go to the register myself. As I stood in line, I started looking forward to Saturday, when I'd be able to go out to eat with Mary and the twins and finally get out of the apartment for a while.

After leaving the store, I drove around for a bit to destress and relax. I hadn't done that much since moving into the apartment. I sipped the Coke I'd bought at the drugstore, driving slowly as the radio played, enjoying the scenery of the woods all around me.

Eventually, I headed back home armed with my new earplugs. The apartment was suspiciously quiet when I entered, as if nothing had happened earlier. I told myself it didn't matter now; at least I had a way to defend myself against the noise. I spent the rest of the evening reading the Bible and praying, asking God especially for peace in the situation with my neighbors and for things to go back to how they had been—quiet and calm.

By nightfall, the apartment had gone entirely silent. Exhausted from the night before, I went to bed early. I drifted off but was awakened again in the early hours by the sound of furniture dragging across the floor above me. Perhaps they were moving out. I glanced at my alarm clock. 4 a.m. Maybe they didn't have time to do it outside of work.

The dragging and stomping continued for nearly an hour. Finally, I put my earplugs in and managed to get a few more hours of sleep. When my alarm went off, I felt more rested than the previous night, having gone to bed earlier. Still, I considered going upstairs to ask the neighbors to quiet down.

I decided it would be better to wait until after work. Showing up that early might seem intrusive, and besides, I didn't know them personally. Talking face-to-face could help the situation. With that thought, I made breakfast and got ready for work, feeling grateful the week had nearly ended. It was finally Friday, and I had Saturday to look forward to. If the neighbors were moving, I reasoned, they'd probably finish over the weekend.

Feeling a little better about everything, I went to work hopeful and ready for my weekend to begin. The day passed quickly.

When I got home that evening, I decided to go up and speak with the neighbors. I knocked on their door. A petite woman with short dark hair answered. She seemed fine at first, open to conversation, but as soon as I mentioned the disturbances I'd been experiencing, her demeanor shifted. She grew defensive and angry, denying any wrongdoing and insisting it had never happened.

I stood there, stunned by her harsh reaction. Then she slammed the door in my face.

I went back to my apartment and finished the last of the lasagna, eating it with a can of ginger ale. The conversation with the neighbors had left me upset, and I prayed to God to take away the hurt and frustration from the situation. As time passed, I started to feel calmer and more focused on relaxing while watching TV.

Not long after, the stomping started again, this time with a louder, heavier dropping noise. I prayed out loud for God to handle the neighbors who seemed to be deliberately disrupting my peace. There wasn't much I could do until I spoke with Brenda.

As I prayed, I heard someone get up from the floor directly above me. It felt as though they had been listening the whole time and left only because I'd started to pray. In that moment, I became sure the neighbor above me was doing this on purpose—making loud noises not only to irritate me but to listen to my reaction as they did it.

I had never experienced anything like this before. I prayed to God for guidance on what to do. I hadn't received an answer yet, so I kept praying. In a strange way, I felt as though these people were driving me closer to God through my prayers.

That night, I read the Bible and listened to prayers I had recorded on a cassette tape. I kept the volume low and let the tape play through the night. Around three a.m., I woke to the sound of loud stomping and objects slamming against the floor above my bed—right above where the cassette tape was playing. I heard the woman get up again from the floor as I prayed out loud for God to help me. For a few minutes, she jumped repeatedly above me, so hard it felt like the ceiling might collapse. Then, as suddenly as it had begun, everything stopped. The apartment went silent for the rest of the night.

The experience left me deeply unsettled. I was beginning to understand what Brenda had been talking about regarding the house. Something had been here; it had left my apartment and gone to the neighbors.

I was just glad it was Saturday morning. After what had happened last night, sleeping in felt like a gift. The apartment above me has been quiet so far this morning.

I got up and made breakfast: strawberry pancakes and tea. A good breakfast hit the spot, and after sleeping in and having a calm morning, I felt much better.

Then Mary called to confirm our plans for dinner tonight. At least I had that to look forward to—finally getting out of the apartment.

I wasn't sure how to spend the rest of the day until dinner. I thought about going to an early movie around 11 AM, just to pass the time and get out of the apartment. After checking the local theater's showtimes, I decided on another comedy. I needed to laugh, stay positive, and keep my faith strong. I reminded myself that God would handle this situation in His way and in His time. Before leaving, I prayed and read the Bible, asking God either to bless me with a new apartment or to bless my neighbor with a new place to live.

When I arrived at the theater, the smell of popcorn hit me right away. I told myself I should pass—especially after strawberry pancakes for breakfast and with dinner coming later—but a small bag couldn't hurt. I bought one along with a large Diet Coke and found my seat. The movie made me laugh, and for a little while, I forgot all about the neighbor.

Afterward, I went grocery shopping for the week, which took up another hour. Back home, I rested, prayed, and read more of the Bible. Then I turned to my novel, jotting down fresh ideas and thinking about some of Edwards' suggestions, deciding whether I wanted to use them. I nearly lost track of time as I wrote, but I set my notes aside to continue later this week.

By then, it was time to get ready for dinner. Excited to go out and spend time with friends, I chose a nice outfit—my black dress with pink Japanese cherry blossoms. I fixed my hair in a bun, clipped in a few cherry blossom pins, and added pink lipstick with matching nail polish. Looking in the mirror, I felt good about myself.

I drove to the restaurant Mary had picked, an upscale Irish pub called Clover's near the downtown square. I arrived first, and Mary came in soon after. As we waited for the twins, she told me more about her breakup and how badly her ex-boyfriend had treated her. I thought it was nice to have someone who understood what I was going through, but at the same time, I wished I had never experienced it myself.

The twins arrived just as the hostess came to seat us. Mary made another remark about her ex, but I didn't catch it because I had already turned to follow the hostess. As we walked, the hostess glanced at the twins and said, almost teasingly, "You've been talking about men the whole time you've been here—how bad they are."

Her tone wasn't sympathetic; it felt mocking. I wished Mary wouldn't discuss this kind of thing in public; it made us seem vulnerable, and in American society, vulnerability is often seen as weakness, something to ridicule rather than respect. I glanced at Mary; her face had gone sad. The twins looked surprised, but none of us said anything. We followed the hostess to our table and opened our menus.

I felt like trying something different, so I kept scanning the options while Mary and the twins chatted. Finally, I settled on the fish and chips and ordered it with a Diet Coke. "Would you all like to go bowling sometime?" I asked. They all agreed, and we picked next Saturday. I noticed Luke looking at me, shy but attentive.

After the meal, the twins left, but Mary and I stayed in the parking lot by our cars. She kept talking about her ex; I could tell she needed someone to listen. "You're sweet to put up with all this," she said.

"You're welcome to talk to me anytime," I told her.

It was past dark by the time I headed home. I had forgotten entirely about the neighbor until the thought crept back in as I drove. I prayed for the apartment to be quiet that night so I could sleep before church in the morning. Christian music played softly on the radio as I pulled into the lot.

The light in the apartment above mine was on. A small sense of dread settled in as I walked toward the lobby. I hoped to see Brenda at the front desk, but she wasn't there.

Inside my apartment, everything was still and quiet. I moved through my nightly routine—changing clothes, making tea. The smell of spicy cinnamon filled the room as I sat on the couch with my cup, turning on the TV to unwind.

Then, suddenly, the neighbor's TV blasted on. I knew she'd heard me come in; she was doing it on purpose. I slipped in my earplugs and ignored it. At some point, she must have turned it off, but I didn't notice. I'd left the earplugs in as I drifted to sleep.

When I woke the next morning, I felt well-rested and content. My alarm read 8 AM.

I made more strawberry pancakes and tea, then sat down to eat breakfast while reading the Sunday newspaper that the residents received each week. I enjoyed browsing through the coupons and reading the funny comics. After finishing, I got ready and went to church.

Lydia was already there, and we talked for a little while. She suggested going out to lunch again, and I proposed next Saturday. It would work, since bowling was scheduled for 5 PM that day. It felt good to plan a full day with friends.

When I returned from church, I saw Brenda in the lobby and told her about the neighbor and everything that had been going on. She asked me to start writing down the days and times of each incident, to keep a log, and to try recording the noise on video. She said she would talk to the neighbor herself and see if that would put a stop to it. I thanked Brenda for her help and went back to my apartment.

The next day at work, we had a crew meeting before starting. Jasper and I were cracking jokes again, and once more, only we laughed at them. Across the circle, I caught Alma looking at me with a menacing expression. There was no kindness in her eyes—only something dark and unexpected, as if she had begun to hate me. I could feel that energy coming off her. When I met her gaze, she quickly looked away and shifted slightly, moving farther from me as if to avoid standing too close, trying to make it look unintentional.

CHAPTER 10

$\mathcal{I}$ fell asleep that Monday night and once again saw, in my dreams, the old familiar figure of Bethany sitting in an empty classroom. One of Jocelyn's friends approached her and asked if she really wanted to fight Jocelyn. Bethany looked stunned. "I never said that," she replied. Another girl—once a fair-weather friend of Bethany's—stepped forward and said she would fight Bethany herself, trying to provoke her as well. Bethany didn't engage. A moment later, the teacher returned to the classroom.

Weeks passed in the dream. Jocelyn's friend, the one who had wanted to fight Bethany, was now telling everyone that Bethany had told the teacher she'd skipped class when, in reality, the girl had been out sick. She spread the false rumor to make Jocelyn happy and ruin Bethany's reputation.

Bethany went home, defeated, and told her mother about the situation. Her mother grew angry. "Where was the teacher while all of this was happening?" she asked. The next day, Bethany's mother said she would go to the school and talk to the teacher herself. Bethany felt a flicker of hope for a good result, but doubted anything would come of it.

The week at work was tense as I navigated my own growing friction with Alma. I ignored it as best I could; she seemed increasingly annoyed with me over small things and had stopped confiding in me about her problems. In a way, her growing distance had been a relief. It gave me time to reflect. She thrived on drama and was clearly seeking it. I also wondered if the timing was connected to the entity I sensed had arrived. Was Alma even aware she might be under its influence? Or would this have been the outcome regardless? There was no way to know for sure.

I had been focusing more on God lately, trying to hear the direction He had for my life. At lunch, I stopped talking so much to Alma and let her be, choosing instead to talk with Jasper and her other friends. I didn't know if it would change anything, but I thought space was needed now more than ever.

By Friday, I was looking forward to the weekend. It was almost time to go home, and I had a whole day planned for Saturday. I cleaned up my unit, put the tarp on, and headed toward my car. For some reason, I felt like Bethany in my dreams. Something about that feeling clicked in my mind.

Am I being shown these dreams for a reason? I wondered. Are they coming from the entity here at Bethany's Well? What is it about this place that draws people in and keeps them here? The questions were piling up faster than I could answer them.

I went back home and fixed myself some tea. Carrying the cup with me, I sat on the couch and glanced out the window. In the parking lot below, the neighbor lady from upstairs stood staring directly at my apartment. I had no idea what she thought she might see, or why she was so intent on looking straight into my windows. She held her gaze even as I looked back at her. I felt myself growing tired of her behavior and wished she would go away. I wondered if she was doing this because Brenda had spoken to her, or if it was simply her own odd habit.

I tried to relax for a while and eventually went to bed early. In the middle of the night, I was awakened again by loud dropping sounds and heavy stomping above my bed. With a sigh, I reached into the nightstand drawer, pulled out my earplugs, and put them in. Soon after, I drifted back to sleep.

I woke naturally in the morning, got up, and made another cup of tea. For breakfast, I wasn't sure what I wanted, so I settled on a peanut butter granola bar with a glass of milk. I didn't want to overeat since I had plans to go out for lunch with Lydia. We had decided on Momma's Kitchen, a convenient spot for both of us.

I spent the morning resting, praying, and reading the Bible. Sitting on the couch in the soft morning light, I let the warmth of the sunshine wash over me. For a moment, I felt peaceful and calm. Then, suddenly, the neighbor upstairs blasted her TV at what had to be full volume—it sounded that way from inside my apartment. I stayed seated, letting the light and warmth of the sun pull me back into peace despite the noise. Even in the most unpleasant situations, I realized, I could choose to rest in that calm.

Soon after, I got ready and headed out for lunch. As I drove closer to the restaurant, hunger set in, and I thought to myself, *I'm definitely going to the right place.* I parked, went inside, and ordered a vanilla chai tea on a whim while I waited.

Lydia walked in a few minutes later, spotted me near the coffee counter, and smiled. She joined me at the table, and we ordered our meals. Over lunch, she talked excitedly about upcoming events at church. Then she leaned forward. "Would you consider teaching Bible school for the little children?"

I smiled back at her. "I'll pray about it and let you know soon."

She nodded in agreement, and we continued talking about the church events as we ate.

I spent the afternoon going on a drive, grabbing a Coke, and relaxing. I took a new route, which led me to a few old bridges and a small, artsy town full of shops and restaurants. I stopped to browse through a couple of jewelry stores and picked up another Coke before realizing the time. It was nearly time to head back for bowling.

The bowling alley was in the downtown square. When I arrived, Mary and the twins were already waiting outside. I parked, walked up to greet them, and together we went in, rented a lane, and got our bowling shoes. Time slipped by as we played, laughing and enjoying ourselves. I even bought a large Coke and a slice of pizza. We ended up playing four rounds, and when the manager offered us one more game for free, we gladly took it.

Afterward, we lingered near the arcade games and benches, talking. Mary shared that she was planning a trip to Greece. We found her itinerary fascinating and discussed it in detail. I thought about how much I would love to travel more.

At one point, I shared with them Lydia's offer for me to become a Bible school teacher for the youth. Their reactions weren't enthusiastic. They began sharing concerns about the church, admitting they had been thinking of leaving for a while. Mary's ex still attended the single young adults' Bible study, and many in the church seemed willing to overlook the way he had wronged her. Mary felt deeply disappointed by that, and I agreed with her.

I turned to her. "If you want to go to another church, I'll support you. What matters is that you stay in your faith and close to God."

Mary smiled at that, and the conversation drifted back to her upcoming trip.

I noticed Luke watching me often as we talked. His attention didn't bother me—I was starting to like it. Still, I tried to act as though I didn't notice, feeling a little shy. Perhaps if he continued to show interest, I would become more comfortable.

Eventually, the evening wound down. Darkness had settled over the square, and it was time for everyone to head home. Luke walked me back to my car, and we exchanged a quick goodnight. For a moment, I thought it might be the perfect opportunity to share my feelings—his actions made it clear he cared about my well-being. Instead, I smiled and told him I would see him at church tomorrow.

He seemed a little disappointed at my abrupt goodnight. Driving away, I couldn't help but wonder if I had let a moment slip by—a moment that might have changed everything. I guessed I would never know for sure.

I got home and decided to go to bed early since I had church in the morning. I turned on my prayer cassette tape at a very low volume, just enough to hear the faint words, and drifted off to sleep quickly.

I was jolted awake by the sound of heavy furniture being dragged across the floor right above my bed again. Then came the loud, repetitive thuds—as if she were picking up ten-pound weights and dropping them from her waist onto the floor. It happened five or six times in a row, followed by a round of stomping that lasted for about ten minutes. Then everything went silent. Completely silent—except for her laughter. Hysterical laughter, echoing through the ceiling for several minutes.

It was an old building, not soundproof like modern ones, but it was still functional. The sounds were unnerving, and the laughter was downright creepy.

I prayed for a while, eventually calming down enough to go back to sleep. When my alarm rang for church, I got up, got ready, and left. Later, after the service, I returned home, tried to rest for the next day, prayed, and read my Bible that afternoon. I baked a frozen pizza for dinner, wrote for a while, then packed my lunch for the morning and went to bed early.

The alarm greeted me the next day with a peaceful melody but a demanding beep that wouldn't stop until I turned it off. I lay there for a few minutes before getting up and starting my routine. As I moved around the apartment, I felt that same unsettling sensation—like I was being watched.

I was nearly ready to leave when I heard it again: a faint laugh, just like the one I'd listened to the day I visited Bethany's Well. The hair on my arms stood on end. I grabbed my purse and work bag and left without looking back.

I drove straight to work, trying to hide my jitters and disbelief over what had just happened. All morning, I kept thinking about that laugh. At lunch, I went through my work bag and realized I'd forgotten my lunch at home. When I told the crew chief, he waved it off. "Go grab something in town," he said. "Or go back home for it—either way, don't worry."

I didn't even consider going back home. Instead, I went to Aurelio's for lunch, remembering their lunch special. It looked far less busy than Momma's Kitchen, which felt like exactly what I needed.

I went inside and ordered Alfredo spaghetti and a Coke. As I waited, the waitress brought me a basket of warm breadsticks. Soon after, my Coke arrived, followed by the entrée. I ate happily—it was delicious—and when I was finished, I left the restaurant feeling complete and ready to get back to work.

As I walked to my car, I heard a faint meow. Looking around, I spotted a dirty white cat with large black spots crouched near my vehicle. He was thin, a little mangy, and clearly filthy. I could tell he was a stray.

"Come here, boy," I called softly from my vehicle.

To my surprise, he came right over. I knelt and petted him, noticing how he stayed close, probably drawn by the smell of food from the restaurant. Feeling sorry for him, I went back inside and ordered a takeout order of meatballs. Outside, I placed the food in front of him, and he devoured it almost instantly.

Right then, I decided to take him with me. I opened my car door, coaxed him in, and started the drive back toward my apartment. On the way, I realized I couldn't take him straight home without supplies. I stopped at a drugstore and bought a litter box, litter, a scoop, and a bag of cat food. I already had disposable plates and bowls at home, so I decided to wait before buying proper food and water bowls.

Driving away from the store, I made up my mind to call him Aurelio—after the restaurant. The name felt right, a way to remember my days as a traveling archaeologist, all the places I'd been, and everything that had happened along the way.

When I got home, I carried the supplies inside first. Then I returned to the car to find Aurelio curled up in the back seat, sleeping without a care in the world. I carefully picked him up so he wouldn't jump out of my arms and carried him inside.

He looked around the apartment, meowing curiously but not upset. I set up a little area for him in the back left corner. He came over to inspect it, clearly approving, and I petted him a bit more before leaving for work.

As I walked to my car, I glanced up at my apartment window. Aurelio was already perched on the windowsill, watching me.

I smiled and drove back to work, thinking about Aurelio for the rest of the day. I didn't tell anyone at my job about finding a stray cat at lunch. It felt like something meant to happen—on one of the rare days I forgot my lunch, there he was at the restaurant I'd chosen. I hadn't even seen a stray cat in Boom Town before.

I went to a local store after work, one with a pet department that was cheaper than the drugstore. I filled my cart with pet shampoo, a brush, food, water dishes, wet cat food, and a collar. I spotted flea and ear mite medication, grabbed it, and then added cat toys and a scratching post. Everything added up quickly, but I felt happy spending it on Aurelio.

When I got back home, I unpacked everything, bathed Aurelio, and applied his flea and ear mite medication. I fastened his new royal blue collar around his neck. "You look so handsome," I told him. He seemed to know it, too.

That night, I let Aurelio roam free while I slept. I slept deeply and woke rested and ready for work. I got dressed, adding a new morning task to my routine—making sure Aurelio was fed and cared for while I was gone.

As I left for work, I glanced up at my window and saw Aurelio watching me again. It tugged at my heart, but it was comforting to know someone was waiting for me at home.

The day passed at work. During lunch, I checked my cell phone and saw a text from a familiar number—Trevor's. It didn't click right away; I'd almost forgotten about him. The message simply said, "HI."

I didn't respond and went back to work. At the end of the day, I drove home, eager to see Aurelio. After making tea, I sat by the window with him when my cell phone rang. Without checking the caller ID, I answered. My stomach dropped at the sound of Trevor's voice saying hello.

He acted as if nothing had happened. I confronted him about blocking me and seeing another woman. He admitted it but added that he didn't want to date her anymore. He didn't seem to understand why I'd be offended at all, insisting I should be happy he'd called for a second chance.

"I'll think about it," I told him. "I need to go."

He said goodnight and hung up. I immediately blocked his number.

My pulse was racing. I didn't even know why. I spent the rest of the evening with Aurelio, then read my Bible and prayed before bed. As I drifted off, I felt God telling me to accept the offer to teach the children's Bible class.

Joy welled up inside me. I wanted to call Lydia and Mary right away to tell them. I even wanted to tell Luke as soon as possible.

I went to sleep feeling truly happy—grateful for God and for my new cat. Aurelio curled up beside me, purring softly. Life felt good. For the first time in a long while, I understood what true contentment and joy felt like. God was wonderful.

CHAPTER 11

The next day at work, I arrived and greeted Alma when she passed by. She ignored me. At first, I thought maybe she hadn't heard me, so I let it go and focused on my morning tasks. I wasn't feeling particularly social anyway; I had a lot to finish before the end of Friday. I noticed Jasper glancing at me a few times as if he wanted to say something. I smiled at him but motioned for him to wait, planning to catch up later. I forgot all about it until lunchtime.

When I went to the usual lunch spot, Jasper was the only one sitting there. "Where is everyone?" I asked.

"They won't be sitting here anymore," he said.

I frowned. "What happened?"

Jasper leaned forward and explained. Alma had admitted she was jealous of our friendship and felt embarrassed about it. She told him she only wanted to share her personal life with him, not with anyone else, and that she wanted his attention throughout the day.

I felt confused and a little hurt by her behavior. "I don't cling to you," I said. "We just have the same sense of humor, and we laugh at things no one else does."

"This morning," Jasper answered when I asked when it all happened.

I nodded slowly. "That explains why she walked past me without saying anything earlier. And I see she took her other two friends with her. It's fine —they never really spoke to me anyway."

Jasper went on. Alma had confided in him, admitting her jealousy, and then started criticizing me, saying I was "this and that" and insisting she didn't want me in the group anymore. She even implied I was hanging around Jasper because I had romantic feelings for him.

I shook my head. "That's not true. I like you as a friend."

"Alma thinks I chose you over her," Jasper said quietly. "But I just made a decision for my own sanity. I don't believe you did anything to cause this."

I sighed. "Maybe I shouldn't have been sitting with the group unless invited."

"I thought it was fine," Jasper replied. "She talked to you, told you things about her personal life. That showed respect."

"I never wanted to cause an issue," I told him. "If Alma thinks I did some-thing wrong, maybe I should talk to her."

Jasper shook his head firmly. "Don't. If she realizes I told you, she'll just be embarrassed. Nothing good will come of it."

I wasn't sure he was right, but he seemed certain. If speaking to her would only make things worse, then I would leave it alone for now.

Jasper seemed to think Alma was mentally ill. He told me he didn't want to be around that kind of behavior anyway. I didn't really believe he had "picked me" the way Alma was blaming me for. It was more than he had lost trust in her and didn't like the way she was acting. I guessed that when she asked him to stop being friends with me, she expected him to shun me, just like her other two friends had done.

I hadn't seen any of this coming, but it happened. I decided I would pray about it and hope things de-escalated. After lunch, I went back to my unit and noticed Alma glaring at me from across the way. I ignored her and spent most of the day talking with Edward instead. Toward the end of the day, I struck up some small talk with Christine, asking how she was doing. She seemed surprised at first but genuinely happy that I'd spoken to her.

When I got home, I found Aurelio curled up on my bed, sleeping peace-fully. He stirred when I walked in, then drifted right back to sleep. Smiling, I made myself some tea and called Lydia. I told her I was happy to accept the teaching offer for the children's Bible class. She was thrilled and said to arrive around 8:30 on Sunday morning so she could go over everything with me, show me the room, and walk me through the lesson plan.

"That sounds great," I told her. "I'll see you Sunday morning."

It felt good to have something positive come from the day.

Later, I called Mary to share the news. Her reaction wasn't as warm. She said, "I hope you like it," in a way that sounded less than enthusiastic. Something in her tone felt off.

"Is everything okay?" I asked.

"Everything's fine," she said quickly. "I'll see you at church on Sunday."

Her response left me confused. I didn't know if she was happy for me or not. I knew she wasn't pleased with the church lately, mostly because of gossip and the way people had handled certain situations, but I didn't know the full story. I chose to focus on the positives instead.

Wanting to wind down after such a long, frustrating day, I drove to Momma's Kitchen for a vanilla chai tea. Sitting there, I thought about Alma. If she had such strong feelings, why hadn't she just spoken to me directly and asked me not to sit with the group? Instead, it felt like she wanted Jasper to prove his loyalty to her by being unkind to me—by treating me badly to make her happy.

I got ready, drove to the restaurant, and went inside to the coffee counter. I ordered a vanilla chai tea and, because it had been such a tough day, a piece of chocolate cake as well.

I sat at a table by the window, sipping my tea and watching people pass by. Then I did a sudden double-take. Trevor was walking right in front of the restaurant. He seemed to be alone and heading toward a bar. For a moment, I remembered how he used to say he spent afternoons collecting payments from his life insurance customers.

The woman working at the counter noticed me staring. "Do you know him?" she asked.

I forced a casual smile. "I just thought he was a guy who sells life insurance," I said, mostly to make small talk.

She shook her head. "No, he isn't. He works as a safety manager for a dumpster company. They supply dumpsters for businesses or homeowners who are renovating."

Her words hit me like a slap. I felt numb. Trevor had lied to me the entire time about his job. He had spun stories about customers, described his days as a life insurance salesman, and I had believed every word. The truth was clear now: he had been a professional liar. You can't build a relationship with someone like that.

I thought about the excuses he had made for never introducing me to his friends or family. He always claimed that things went downhill the moment he introduced girlfriends to them. But maybe the truth was more straight-forward—perhaps they just knew he was a liar and told the truth about him.

Anger and irritation flared inside me. A part of me wanted to follow him into that bar and confront him, to finally give him a piece of my mind. But I stopped myself. Now I understood why this man had been pulling me away from God, and I saw clearly how the Lord had prospered me by ending that relationship. Trevor was staying blocked.

Life, I was learning, is simpler than I used to think. The key is to focus on making God happy, not people. When you live for God, you reflect Jesus, and that reflection protects you. It keeps you from getting entangled with people who don't have your best interests at heart—people who only want to use you for their selfish needs. Anyone who asks you to do wrong never truly cares for you; they only seek their own gain and, ultimately, your destruction.

At least now I knew what kind of person Trevor was. I could pray for the Lord to bring me the right one. I felt happy to be over Trevor and ready to move on with my life. I sipped my tea at the restaurant and finished my cake. With nowhere in particular to be, I thought about what I should do next. I could go home and write, but after seeing Trevor that afternoon and discovering his dishonesty, I didn't feel like being alone. It wasn't my shame for being lied to—it was his. Still, we should always pray for discernment. On our own, we are easily deceived, but God is omnipresent, full of wisdom, and knows everything. He knows what lies in every heart, what people are planning, and their intent in every situation.

I decided to order dinner. The waitress laughed and said, "Dessert first, huh?" I smiled and ordered barbecue ribs, French fries, and a Coke. As I ate, I couldn't help feeling sad, wishing I had been smarter about Trevor. But I reminded myself of what God tells us: people will lie because they are of the world. "But you are not of the world. Take comfort, for I have conquered the world. Lean on my understanding, and I will guide you." Those words steadied me.

I began to feel better and thought about going home to read the Bible, pray, and, of course, spend time with Aurelio. A pet was a far better investment of love and energy than a bad boyfriend. A pet gave love freely and wanted to be part of your life without the selfish conditions of a man like Trevor.

When I got home, I rested for the evening. I was glad the week was nearly over and that tomorrow would be Friday. I played with Aurelio, holding a feather toy on a string as he chased it around the apartment. Later, I made a cup of tea, prayed, and read the Bible. When I went to bed, Aurelio curled up beside me again.

The next morning, I woke to the sound of an angry alarm. It was definitely a Friday. I dragged myself out of bed and made breakfast: toast with peanut butter and a glass of milk. Then I fixed Aurelio's plate of wet food, and he gobbled it down happily.

I headed to work thinking about how much I wanted Saturday to be here already, and what I could do tomorrow to get away for the day. Maybe I'd explore a new place I hadn't been before.

As I drove, I thought about my options. I could visit a state park or explore a small town. I'd heard there was a historic mill nearby. "I think I'll see it tomorrow," I murmured to myself.

Pulling into the parking area, I went to my unit and saw Christine. "Hi," I said as I passed. She looked busy, already working. Jasper arrived a little later, followed by Edward. A while after, I noticed Alma from afar. She was glaring at me again. As her eyes locked on mine, I heard it—the same creepy laughter from Bethany's Well.

I glanced around. No one. The sound chilled me. I decided then that on Monday I'd bring another disposable camera to work. The next time I heard the laughing, I'd start taking pictures in the direction it came from.

I kept glancing over my shoulder as I worked. The laughter came again, this time joined by whispering. I turned, heading to get the camera to photograph my finished level, and then I saw it.

A tall, demon-like entity stood briefly before me. I blinked, and it was gone. My papers fluttered on the clipboard as if a gust of wind had passed, but there was no breeze. It felt as though whatever I had seen had walked quickly past me, stirring the air.

After that, I was ready to go home for the weekend. I was almost sure I'd just seen whatever Brenda claimed she'd seen in her house. I wanted to speak with her, to get the full story and find out who or what this presence was and why it stayed at Bethany's Well. Once I had a picture at work, I planned to show Brenda the photo from Bethany's Well alongside the one from here and ask her what she had seen.

It scared me, the way there was no kindness in Alma's eyes anymore—only an intense, hateful stare. I believed she was being influenced by the entity lingering around Bethany's Well. Still, I reminded myself she didn't have to listen to it. We all have a choice in what we allow into our lives. That's why, when evil thoughts come into our minds and we rebuke them, they go away.

I went home and put a frozen pizza in the oven. Aurelio wanted some, so I gave him a pepperoni slice, but he only pushed it around on his plate with his right paw. I finished the pizza, watched TV for a while, and then went to bed early so I could get up and head to the historic mill in the morning.

Sometime later, I woke up around 3 a.m.—unusual for me. I tried to go back to sleep, but then I heard footsteps in the apartment. My body froze with fear. I lay as still as I could, as if being motionless would make me invisible. Then I heard someone sit down on the couch.

I forced myself to look. Slowly, I turned over and sat up slightly, but there was no one there. Still, I had clearly heard it—the footsteps moving around, the couch creaking, the cushion sinking as if under a person's weight. Brenda had said I might come to understand what she'd been talking about, and now I thought I was beginning to—whether I wanted to or not.

When morning came, I realized I hadn't set my alarm. I woke after 10 a.m. and couldn't help but wonder if I had truly forgotten—or if whatever had been there in the night had turned it off. I would never know. I made strawberry pancakes with tea, then considered whether I still had time to see the mill. In the end, I decided to stay home, write, and run my weekly errands. The mill could wait until next weekend.

The day passed, and I went to bed ready for Sunday morning. I woke early, prepared for church, and felt an unusual urgency—as though I should run straight there. Instead, I stopped for breakfast at Momma's Kitchen. I ordered my usual tea along with two chocolate donuts topped with coconut sprinkles. Sitting down at a small table, I ate in silence.

I arrived at church at exactly 8:30 a.m. and met Lydia in the foyer. She showed me to the classroom and went over the rules, procedures, and lesson plans. I would be working with a co-teacher and starting the following week. Lydia just wanted me to get familiar with everything beforehand. With the children's Bible study growing, a second classroom was needed to accommodate everyone.

I WAS a little disappointed I couldn't start this week, but it was fine—I could begin next week. In the hallway, I saw Mary and the twins. I waved and said hello, and they came over. I told them about the new Children's Bible study class.

Mary asked how everything was going. I admitted, "Trevor texted me again."

She frowned. "What are you going to do about it?"

"Nothing," I said. "I just blocked him again."

Mary studied me closely. "Do you still have feelings for him?"

I sighed. "I wish he had been a better person. It might have worked out."

When I glanced at Luke, I noticed the hurt in his eyes. My words had landed wrong. I hadn't meant to hurt him, but I could tell I had, and I didn't know how to take it back.

We stood talking for a while before going into the service. I sat beside Mary, with the twins on her other side. As the sermon went on, I thought about asking if they wanted to go out for lunch afterward.

When the service ended, though, they all stood quickly. The twins explained they had to get to work, and Mary said she needed to catch up on chores at home. I forced a smile, though disappointment tugged at me. "Alright. I'll see you next week."

As they walked away, I remembered the young adults' Bible study class. They had skipped it today. I just stood there, watching them leave the sanctuary, with the strange, unsettled feeling that something had ended—though I couldn't say what.

CHAPTER 12

I stopped by the drugstore on the way home and picked up a disposable camera. I planned to keep it at work among my supplies. I decided to buy two, just in case one broke or I needed to take a lot of pictures. After checking out, I headed back to my car and drove home, where I made myself some tea.

For a while, I just watched TV, processing everything that had happened. It was the first time since arriving in Boom Town that I had truly rested. For once, I didn't feel the need to stay constantly moving and busy. Later, I wrote more in my novel and then gathered my clothes basket and detergent to do laundry.

As I shut my apartment door, I noticed Thomas leaving. "Hi," he said as he passed by.

"Hi," I replied with a small smile.

He turned back toward me. "Would you like to go out to dinner sometime? I got a gift card for my birthday from work. I don't go to the restaurant much, so I'll never spend it all."

I smiled. "I'd love to."

"Next Saturday would be a good time for me," he said.

"That's good for me too," I replied.

We said goodbye, and he went on his way while I stayed to do my laundry.

That night, I fell asleep and slipped into another lucid dream. I saw Bethany walking in the woods. It looked like late fall—some leaves still clung to the trees, but the air felt cold, and she wore a long red coat. I could never see her face in these dreams, only the back of her head with her long, black hair curled at the ends.

Bethany was hurrying to get home. She had run a few errands in town for her mother and was cutting through the woods to take a shortcut. Worry crept over her that it might get dark before she made it back. She wondered if she had made a mistake coming this way.

As she walked, she saw a group of people in a circle off the path, chanting softly. She slowed, curiosity and unease mixing in her chest. She didn't want to pry, but the path led closer to them. As she neared, she began to make out faint whispers—and what she understood was not good.

They were casting a spell.

Bethany's eyes widened as she passed and recognized Jocelyn beneath a hooded coat. Jocelyn looked back at Bethany, her eyes dark and steady. A whisper rose from the circle—someone saying, "We should kill her for seeing us here today."

Bethany didn't recognize the voice, but terror flooded her. She quickened her pace, moving as fast as she could to get away.

Bethany heard footsteps pounding behind her and bolted for a hiding place. She knew of a hollow tree just off the path, its solid side facing outward. A few people realized that the tree was hollow from the back. She sprinted toward it, slipped inside, and covered herself with nearby branches. Her heart pounded as she whispered a desperate prayer. "God, please save me."

Minutes crawled by. She wanted to leave, but something inside urged her to stay hidden. Then she saw one of the men from the group walk past. He didn't seem to notice her at all, though she was partially visible in her red coat. He should have seen her—but it was as if she were invisible. From that day on, Bethany began attending church, convinced that God had saved her. She knew those men would return to kill her soon, but she never forgot the moment she had been spared.

The next morning, I went to work as usual, bringing the cameras with me. I focused on my tasks and spent the day chatting with coworkers in my unit. I didn't recall seeing Alma at all that day. The cameras stayed tucked away in my supply bucket. I didn't ignore the fact they were there—I simply left them untouched.

When I got home, there was a note taped to my door saying maintenance had been in the apartment. I hadn't been told they were coming. As I opened the door, I expected Aurelio to run to me, but he didn't. Panic rising, I searched the apartment from top to bottom but couldn't find him. My heart sank. The note on the door, Aurelio's absence; it all came together. Maintenance must have let my cat out.

In a panic, I called Brenda. My voice trembled as I explained what had happened. She came over at once, and together we searched outside Rosario House, calling Aurelio's name over and over.

I walked the parking lot and the surrounding grounds, feeling sick. I had no idea what I would do if he stayed out all night. Brenda suggested I set Aurelio's litter box by the front door to help draw him back and said she'd make flyers to post around.

By nightfall, I went back inside empty-handed. Aurelio was still missing. I spent the rest of the night praying, stepping outside every so often to check for him, and calling friends to ask for prayers. Finally, I went to bed early, determined to wake before daybreak and search again with a flashlight.

I went to bed, but sleep was hard to find. Knowing Aurelio was out there alone, vulnerable to anything, left me restless. I prayed over and over for his safe return. The apartment felt empty without him, and I could do nothing but worry.

When morning came, I dragged myself to work feeling hollow. Jasper noticed immediately. "What's wrong?" he asked.

"Maintenance came by yesterday," I said, my voice tight. "They left the door open. My cat got out."

Jasper frowned. "I'm sorry. If he doesn't come back in a few days, though...he probably won't. That's just been my experience. They're so small, they don't get a good look at things the way we do, so it's hard for them to find their way." He paused. "Still, I hope he does come back."

I nodded, unable to answer. All I could do was pray as I worked, begging God to lead Aurelio home.

At lunch, Jasper asked, "Does your cat have a microchip? Or at least a collar?"

"He has a collar," I admitted, "but I haven't had a chance to take him to the vet yet for a microchip." The guilt hit me hard. "I should've been more proactive."

"Don't blame yourself," Jasper said. "A microchip or a collar doesn't guarantee you'll find him anyway."

I sat in silence, staring down at the table, my thoughts tangled around Aurelio. I hadn't realized how much I loved him until he was gone, and I'd only had him for such a short time. When lunch ended, I went back to work, but I couldn't focus. Inside, I felt lost.

Going home was worse than I expected. The silence of the apartment struck me immediately. I stepped outside again, calling for Aurelio and searching the parking lot and nearby trees.

My phone rang. Brenda's voice came through, hopeful. "Did you find Aurelio yet?"

"No," I said, my throat tight. "I'm looking right now."

Her voice faltered with disappointment, but she quickly added, "I'll keep praying for him—and for you too. You'll be reunited soon."

"Thank you," I whispered before hanging up and continuing the search.

Outside, Thomas spotted me. "What's going on?" he asked.

"I lost Aurelio," I told him. "He slipped out when maintenance came."

Thomas helped me look for a while. As we walked, he said, "I'll pray for you to find him."

"Do you go to church?" I asked quietly.

"Yes," he said. "It's a small church a few miles from here."

We talked as we searched, and he told me he worked as a contractor in home remodeling and liked to play the guitar in his free time. After a while, we said good night and went back to our apartments.

Inside, I sat on the couch with a cup of tea, still praying. I tried to relax, but it felt wrong. Aurelio was still out there—lost, alone—and until he came back, I wouldn't find peace.

The next day at work, I heard laughter just as I was about to take lunch near my unit. I pulled out the disposable camera and snapped a few pictures in the direction of the sound. The laughter grew closer, so I took more shots. Thankfully, no one was around to see me—everyone else had already gone to lunch. I had stayed behind to finish paperwork before eating.

Since the film was used up, I decided to take the camera home with me. I didn't want to leave it unattended overnight, so I slipped it into my work bag. On the way home, I dropped it off at the same drugstore for developing. As before, I would have to wait a week for the results, but I had high hopes this time. Maybe I would finally have proof of a demonic entity lingering around Bethany's Well.

Saturday arrived, and it was time for dinner with Thomas. He knocked on my door, holding a small bouquet. Smiling, he handed it to me, and I was genuinely surprised. He was dressed nicely—something Trevor had never bothered to do. Thomas walked me out to the parking lot, where we each took our own cars and met again at the restaurant.

We chose Momma's Kitchen, and the hostess seated us near the fireplace. We shared a warm meal and spent the entire time talking. When the bill came, Thomas paid in cash.

"I thought you had a gift card," I said, raising an eyebrow.

"I did," he admitted. "But it was for Aurelio's Restaurant. After Aurelio went missing, I knew you wouldn't want to eat there until he was found. You told me all that while we were looking for him together. I remembered."

His words struck me. He actually listened. He cared about how I felt.

Smiling, I suggested, "Why don't we have a cup of coffee or tea and share a slice of cake? My treat."

Thomas agreed, and we moved to a table in front of the coffee counter. We lingered there for a long while, still talking, until the restaurant finally shut down for the night. Back at Rosario House, we chatted a little more in the parking lot before saying goodnight—though not before we did one last search for Aurelio.

The next morning, I made strawberry pancakes again and brewed some tea before heading out for my first day of Children's Bible Study. I met the co-teacher, a kind woman who had been leading the class for years. She took the lead and showed me how to manage the project. I had fun, and I thought I would genuinely enjoy it going forward.

When I arrived at the sanctuary for the sermon, I noticed Mary and the twins weren't there. I went to the young adult Bible study afterward, and again, they were absent. After church, I decided to call Mary; it seemed strange that none of them had shown up.

She answered, but her voice was cold and distant. She told me they had begun attending a new church. She didn't say where, nor did she share any details, only that if they liked it, they wouldn't be coming back to ours.

Her words stung. I would have expected at least a goodbye without having to reach out myself to find out what was going on. It was clear she wanted to cut ties, leaving no way for me to contact her in the future—a phone number can be blocked easily enough.

I realized then I had been right when I felt something had ended, but I couldn't put my finger on it. They were gone. I had no choice but to let go of Luke as well. I still felt a pang of regret, since I had seen potential for a relationship, but if he had truly cared for me, he would have done what Thomas did—he would have asked me out.

That morning, as I fixed breakfast, I glanced at the bouquet Thomas had given me, still sitting in its vase on the coffee table.

The following week passed quickly, much of it spent talking with Thomas. On Friday night, I stayed up late finishing a TV movie. Just as it ended, I heard a faint meow at my door. When I opened it, Aurelio was sitting there.

Tears welled up as I scooped him into my arms. I hugged him tightly, overwhelmed. Somehow, I knew God had brought him back. How else could he have gotten into the lobby unless he slipped through behind someone entering or leaving? It felt like pure mercy—a minor miracle.

I noticed how dirty he was, so I drew him a bath. He protested loudly, meowing and clawing at the tub in his attempt to escape. He clearly hated the smell of the shampoo. But as the grime washed away, Aurelio transformed from a dusty gray cat into the white kitty with large black spots I had first known. Smiling, I whispered, "I can finally recognize you again."

That night, I called everyone to share the news. They were all overjoyed that he was back home safe. I promised to take him to the vet soon to get him microchipped. Holding him close, I felt my faith deepen. God had shown me His mercy, reminding me that He is faithful.

The next morning, I went into town to pick up the film. Back in my car, I opened the envelope and began to look through the photos, eager to see what they had captured. I was shocked by what I saw, too.

In one of the first pictures, a strange man appeared—a man with a large nose and a face that wasn't quite human, yet still eerily human-like. He stood at a distance, watching me as I took his picture, and he seemed to be smiling. It was the same direction from which I had heard the laughing.

As I flipped through more pictures, I realized there weren't just one but two distinct figures. They looked almost like tall goblins, with exaggerated features and pointed, tinted ear tips. The original image truly had captured two men, or rather, two beings.

The most shocking images, though, were the ones of Alma. I hadn't realized at the time that she had been eating lunch in a new spot I didn't know about. Through the trees, I could see her sitting—most likely on a bucket—while one of the goblin-like entities stood behind her, appearing to speak.

No one else could see these entities, but they were there. Even if others couldn't hear the laughter like I could, the beings were still speaking to them —on some level, making their presence known, seeping into their subconscious minds.

I decided I would take the photos to Brenda soon and show her what I had found. I was certain something was at Bethany's Well. I didn't know what Brenda would say, but I was convinced this was connected to Rosario House. Bethany's dreams were somehow linked to these entities.

And now, I couldn't help wondering—was I becoming the new Bethany in this situation? Look at how Alma had turned on me out of nowhere over something I hadn't done to her. The same thing had happened to Bethany with Jocelyn.

I still had no idea why these entities were here or what they wanted. Maybe there was another backstory behind them, something hidden. I hoped I would find out more soon when I spoke with Brenda.

Since I was already in town at the drug store, I decided to stop by Momma's Kitchen for my usual tea and a couple of chocolate and coconut donuts. As I ate, I thought about what to do with the rest of my day and looked forward to going to church tomorrow. I considered visiting the historic mill, though I wasn't sure.

Before I could decide, my phone rang. It was Thomas.

"Hey," he said, "a couple of my friends are taking the boat out on the lake. Want to come fishing with us?"

I hesitated, then smiled. "Sure."

"I can drive if you want to just take one car," he offered.

"That works," I replied.

After we hung up, I headed back to the apartment to get ready. I packed a sun hat, sunscreen, a few bottles of water, and some cans of Coke.

I had only been fishing a handful of times as a child, along the bank of a river. This would be my first time fishing from a boat. It would also be my first time meeting some of Thomas's close friends. Unlike Trevor, I could already tell Thomas would bring me a very different kind of experience.

When I finished getting ready, I met Thomas in the parking lot, and we drove together to the lake. The ride was beautiful, surrounded by forest, and the water itself sparkled with the reflection of the trees along its edge.

At the dock by Chip's house, Thomas introduced me to his best friend, Chip, and Chip's girlfriend, Lacy. Chip shook my hand warmly. "I've heard a lot about you," he said with a smile, glancing between Thomas and me.

Thomas moved a little closer as we stood there talking, and I couldn't help but smile back at him.

CHAPTER 13

On Sunday, I attended church as usual. I really enjoyed the children's Bible study class; we worked on fun art projects tied to the weekly message. Still, I found myself looking around occasionally, half hoping Mary or the twins might show up. I began to wonder whether I should invite Thomas to my church or visit his instead.

When I got home, I thought about how to bring up the conversation with Brenda regarding the pictures. Honestly, I wasn't sure how to do it. I prayed about it, but no clear answer came.

That afternoon, I decided to rest at home. I spent some time with Aurelio, writing for a while. For lunch, I made a macaroni and cheese casserole—my favorite. I planned to use the leftovers for work lunches over the next few days.

Brenda was still on my mind, and I considered leaving her a note at the receptionist's desk, asking her to call me. But the thought of it felt awkward. Instead, I eventually sent her an email with the picture of the smiling goblin attached, asking if she knew anything about Bethany's Well.

It felt strange and uncomfortable, but at least it gave her an easy way to ignore the question if she wanted to. If I confronted her directly, she might feel pressured to say something—or worse, freeze up and resent me later. I didn't want Brenda to feel forced into a conversation she wasn't ready for.

With that settled, I turned back to the rest of my day. I had more maca-roni and cheese casserole for dinner, and then ended the evening with prayer and Bible reading. With nothing else to do, I went to bed early, deter-mined to start the week rested and focused.

On Monday, I went to work as usual and arrived at my unit ready for the new week. Jasper wasn't there. I couldn't explain it, but I knew something had happened—not necessarily something bad, but I had a strong feeling he wasn't coming back.

I stayed focused, chatting briefly with Edward and Christine throughout the day. At lunch, I sat by myself near my unit. Tomorrow, I will try to find a better spot, but for now, I'm not asking anyone to join me.

I had expected to eat my lunch in a somber, solemn mood, remembering Jasper and all the good jokes we used to share. Suddenly, Edward and Chris-tine came over and sat beside me as if this had been their habit all along. I was glad for their company and enjoyed talking with them; it took my mind off everything that had been happening. I hadn't expected them to sit with me, at least not so soon.

At the end of the day, I found a note tucked inside my paperwork in the storage clipboard. It was from Jasper.

Hi, Calina,

I'm transferring to a new pipeline project. I didn't want to tell anyone until after I left, except Derek, the crew chief, who already knew about my transfer request. It's gotten too awkward working here with Alma. I hope you understand. If you're interested, I can also try to get you on this project. My phone number is on the back of this note. I hope to stay in touch.

Jasper

I felt numb reading the letter. I had thought we were better friends than this. I would have expected him to tell me in person. Still, I was happy for him—he'd gotten a new job. A transfer actually sounded like a great idea, considering everything going on here. I might even transfer later.

But if I transferred, I'd probably lose my apartment and any chance at a relationship with Thomas, at least initially. The thought made me hesitate.

I slipped the note into my work bag to take home. As I left work, I told myself I didn't want to go home yet. I needed time to process it all. Losing

Jasper at work would be hard; without him, it felt like I had no one there who really cared about me anymore.

I didn't want to bring it up to Thomas yet—especially not anything about Alma. I liked to keep my work life separate from my personal life. Besides, what if he judged me, thinking I'd done something to Alma? What if he didn't take my side?

For now, I would keep it to myself. Instead, I thought about going to Momma's Kitchen for one of their seasonal ice cream cones. Summer was almost over. I should try it soon anyway.

I drove there and went inside. I ordered two scoops of mint chocolate chip in a waffle cone and carried it outside to one of the tables. As I ate my ice cream, I noticed a young woman sitting on a bench, looking at me.

She was staring at me with pure hatred, as if I'd run her over with my car and kept going. Her expression was strangely familiar. Then I glanced beside her and saw Alma. A small group of people sat with them, likely relatives. Maybe they were all going out to eat and waiting for someone to arrive; there were plenty of restaurants nearby.

The young woman kept fixing me with that deliberately menacing stare. I found it irritating. She clearly thought I cared about her contempt, but I didn't—not about whatever Alma might have told her about me. What I did find ridiculous was how the whole issue refused to die. People who seek to be offended will always find a way. I had never meant anyone harm or acted with bad intentions just by wanting to sit with them at lunch. Yet here I was, staring at the fallout.

I looked back at her without showing anger, but I could feel something inside me shift. I wasn't mad—not really—but somehow, being around these people had begun to change my emotions. My anger felt inflated, unnatural. How were they doing this? How were they making me feel something that wasn't mine?

"Calina!" Thomas's voice cut through my thoughts.

I turned as he walked up beside me. "I saw you from across the street," he said with a smile. "I wanted to come over and say hi."

"That's very nice of you," I said. "How are you doing?"

"I'm doing well," Thomas replied. "I'm glad to see you. Want to get dinner here? My treat."

I agreed, and as I spoke with him, the anger drained completely from my body. I glanced back toward the bench. Alma and her family were gone. I looked around. They had disappeared in under a minute.

Thomas had no idea what had just happened. He chatted easily about his day, even mentioning that I'd soon meet his family at their upcoming barbecue.

"That's a great idea," I said. "I'm glad our relationship is progressing so much lately."

He smiled. "Maybe we could meet your family soon?"

"That's a good idea," I told him. "I'll discuss it with them soon."

Thomas asked about my work and about Aurelio. I mentioned that Jasper was leaving for a new project. He seemed surprised, wondering why anyone would walk away from a good phase three project. I didn't answer. Instead, I discreetly changed the subject. A moment later, I regretted it; I had lost an opportunity to see how Thomas might react and whether he would support me in the situation.

Thomas smiled as we shifted to lighter talk, suggesting we go back to the lake to fish. He wanted to go again that weekend. I agreed, and he seemed genuinely happy.

Afterward, we walked around the downtown square, still talking. Thomas told me he enjoyed horseback riding and wanted to take me into the mountains. He mentioned the beautiful trails, and I admitted I was eager to see the mountains of Arkansas anyway.

"You're right," I told him. "You already know me very well."

That comment caught his attention. He studied me for a moment, as if wondering what I meant about knowing him. But he followed my lead when I dropped the subject and moved on. I could still tell the thought lingered in his mind.

On Saturday morning, I woke up and made breakfast. I wanted an omelet, so I poured myself a glass of orange juice. I thought about calling Jasper, asking how he was doing and what had really made him leave. For now, though, I decided against it. If Jasper had wanted to talk to me, he would have.

I spent part of the morning on the couch with Aurelio curled up beside me, a cup of tea in hand, and my notebook open. I considered turning on the TV for the news or a movie, but then the woman upstairs began stomping around again, blasting her television. I sighed. It was a beautiful day outside, so I could get out. Staying here would only frustrate me.

I didn't know exactly where to go, so I thought about visiting the historic mill I'd wanted to see for a while. The idea sounded pleasant. I got ready, made sure Aurelio had enough food and water, and left.

The drive was long but lovely, winding through forest-lined roads. The mill stood in a small town filled with historic homes, each with neat gardens and manicured yards lined by sidewalks. I drove around for a while just to take it in. I wished I lived in a town like this, with a little garden of my own.

Before heading home, I noticed several restaurants and thought about stopping for lunch. A nice meal would do me good.

I finally arrived at the long-awaited historic mill. It was beautiful—a small but picturesque wooden building dating back to the mid-1800s, nestled among quiet woods. I parked my car and walked toward the ticket booth, but for some reason, I ended up wandering the grounds first instead of buying a ticket.

As I looked around, something caught my eye. A few people were walking among the trees. One woman wore a striking red coat, and I watched as the small group moved slowly, their steps deliberate. They seemed to be forming a circle.

A chill ran through me. What if the dream I'd had was real? What if people really were still performing rituals around Bethany's Well? Could this somehow be connected to the entity I'd sensed at Bethany's Well and Boom Town?

I decided then to go back to Bethany's Well the following afternoon. I needed to look more closely, to see if there were signs of people in the woods. I didn't know what I would find, but I felt compelled to try.

I went back to the ticket booth, bought my admission, and toured the lovely mill.

Afterward, I stopped at one of the little restaurants in town—a cozy log cabin serving breakfast and lunch all day. I ordered country-fried steak with mashed potatoes. Sitting there, I wished I had come to see the mill with Thomas.

When I got home, the apartment was quiet. My mind drifted back to

Bethany's Well, to the strange energy there, to my dreams. I opened my laptop to check my email and saw a message from Brenda. She wanted to talk soon about the picture and the Rosario House. An ominous feeling washed over me.

I wrote back, asking when she would be available to talk, thinking carefully about how to bring up the connection to Rosario House. With a cup of tea in my hand, I told myself she would probably take a day or two to reply.

I spent the rest of the evening watching TV, then praying and reading the Bible before bed. I went to sleep early, planning to attend church in the morning.

Sometime in the night, I woke suddenly to the sound of knocking at my window. Three knocks. I didn't know how long it had been going on before I woke, but three was all I heard.

I stayed awake for a while after hearing the knocks. Part of me wanted to get up and see who was at the window, but I hesitated. It could have been a dangerous person. Maybe it had nothing to do with the entity or Bethany's Well at all—just a random person knocking to find someone, or a prank by local kids. I didn't know.

Eventually, I fell back asleep and was awakened by the sound of my alarm clock. I got up, got ready for church, and made a simple breakfast: toast with peanut butter and a glass of milk. Aurelio ran around the house while I ate. I hugged him and fed him a can of wet food for his Sunday morning treat.

Then came another knock—this time at the door. I looked through the peephole and saw Brenda. I opened the door and greeted her. She stepped inside, looking anxious.

"Is everything okay?" I asked.

"Yes," she said quickly. "I just wanted to talk about your email."

We sat down on the couch, and she began her story.

"When I was very little," Brenda said, "my parents bought Rosario House for far less than it was worth. After a while, we learned why. There was a strange man who lingered around the house. He'd make his presence known by playing games. An Ouija board would appear out of nowhere and tell my sister and me awful things—especially about its contempt for Christians."

She paused, then continued. "At first, we thought it was just our imaginations. We had no idea something truly sinister was there. The man called himself a 'Jack of all trades'—but what he really did was turn people against each other, make them hate one another. It's not a man at all. It's a demon, and it's playing a game to harm people."

Brenda explained that her parents were Christians and, through intense prayer and fasting, had managed to drive it from the house for a long time. "Most likely," she said, "one of the tenants has brought it back—summoned it—or it's followed someone here."

A wave of nausea and dread rolled through me. Brenda noticed my reaction and tried to reassure me. "Jack can be evicted again from Rosario House," she said softly. "We've done it before."

I felt a little better at her words, but the weight of what she'd told me still pressed down on me. For the first time, I felt genuinely uncomfortable living in my apartment.

Brenda told me it would be okay and that she would help me get rid of Jack. I felt a little better and thanked her. As she left, she smiled. "I'll be in touch soon. We'll come up with another game plan to deal with Jack." Then she was gone.

I stayed in my apartment for a while, but then I remembered I needed to get ready for church. I left and made it to the children's Bible study just in time. Still, I wasn't very focused. My mind kept drifting back to what Brenda had said about Jack. It left me feeling sad and heavy. But I tried to remind myself of the truth—that Jesus had already won the victory. I only needed to focus on him, and he would handle the rest. In fact, I had begun to realize that my goal should be to make God happy, not people. If God were pleased with me, everything else would fall into place.

After Bible study, I went to the sermon in the sanctuary. I found myself glancing around for Mary and the twins, though they weren't there. I did spot Lydia sitting with her family, but she hardly noticed me. A wave of loneliness passed over me. I wish Thomas were here. Maybe I'd invite him next week or visit his church instead.

I listened to the sermon and then attended the adult singles class. Still, I couldn't help but feel out of place. If things worked out with Thomas, I wouldn't need this class anyway, especially since the people there seemed judgmental about my clothes and quick to size me up by how much money I had.

When I returned home, a bouquet was waiting at my door. Just then, Thomas's door creaked open, and he stepped out as I bent to pick them up. He smiled. "How was church this morning?"

I smiled back, holding the flowers. "Good," I said, telling him about my morning—though I left out the part about Brenda.

"Want to grab lunch?" he asked.

I nodded, and my smile widened. "I'd like that."

Thomas offered me his arm, and I slipped my hand through as we walked outside together.

CHAPTER 14

That night, I went to sleep and dreamed of Bethany. I saw her walking past the well near the cabin before stepping inside, the place where she lived. She had no idea the two young men from the group who had chased her that day were watching from the edge of the trees.

They crept toward the well. One of them pulled a vial of poison from his pocket, something he had grabbed on a whim. Snickering, they poured it into the water, convinced she would drink it soon—and even better, perhaps her whole family would as well.

What they didn't know was that Bethany had already fetched water for the day. At that moment, she was alone in the cabin, her family away. Her parents and brother had been discussing a move to Boston, where her father hoped to open a barber shop and her mother dreamed of starting a seamstress business. The true reason, though, was Bethany herself. They wanted her to attend a good high school, to learn a trade, or perhaps become a nurse or a teacher. They knew she was miserable in Boom Town and longed for her to have a brighter future.

Her grandmother had come to watch over her while they were gone. Bethany felt safe with her, especially as they cooked together in the kitchen. She listened with comfort to her grandmother's stories about growing up on the frontier.

Meanwhile, the young men slunk away, laughing, certain they had rid themselves of Bethany once and for all. They skipped off to boast to the others about what they had done.

Not long after, Jocelyn and a few of her school friends passed by the cabin. Thirsty from their walk, they glanced around, saw no one outside, and headed for the well. Bethany and her grandmother, busy inside, never noticed. The girls pulled up a bucket and drank freely, smirking as if they had stolen something trivial from an enemy.

They returned to Jocelyn's house for afternoon tea, unaware of what was already taking root inside them.

Later that day, there was a knock at Bethany's door. She opened it to find a police officer standing there.

"Bethany," he said gravely, "I need to ask you a few questions."

She frowned, puzzled. "What's going on? I've been here all day with my grandmother."

The officer shifted uncomfortably. "Jocelyn and her schoolmates have been found dead. Poisoning. Some in the community believe it was you."

Bethany's eyes widened. "Me? How could they think that?"

"They claim you poisoned your own well, hoping to poison the town," the officer explained.

She shook her head in disbelief. "Why would I poison my own well? That's my only source of water. Why would I try to kill the entire town? What reason would I have? What motive could I possibly have for such an act?"

The officer shifted his weight and spoke carefully. "Some in the community think you were jealous of Jocelyn. She was rich, beautiful, popular—well-loved by everyone."

Bethany straightened. "She might have been all those things," she said, "but that still doesn't explain why I would poison the rest of the town."

He paused, frowning. "No," he admitted. "It doesn't explain it at all. Not as a motive for attempting to kill the whole town."

With that, he tipped his hat and left.

Bethany's grandmother went outside to look around. She walked up to the well and saw the bucket sitting on the edge, knowing it had been used and left there. Bethany stepped out as well and noticed something glinting in the grass—a gold heart necklace Jocelyn often wore. She picked it up, staring at it in her palm.

With the necklace and the bucket, both of them knew the truth: Jocelyn and her friends had been there and had drunk from the poisoned water.

"Who could have done such a thing?" Bethany asked her grandmother. "And why?"

Her grandmother's face was grim. "What's important is our safety right now. I think leaving for Boston immediately is in our best interest. No one knows we've been planning to move there."

Bethany hesitated. "But maybe it's better to stay and clear this up."

"That could be risky," her grandmother warned. "If the town really believes you poisoned your own well to kill them off…"

Bethany fell silent, unsure what to do. Her grandmother said nothing more, both of them standing there in the quiet until a sound broke the still-ness—low, mocking laughter from the woods.

They exchanged a glance and slowly walked closer to the tree line. A figure stepped out of the shadows—a twisted goblin-like creature with sharp eyes and a crooked smile.

"Who…who are you?" Bethany asked, her voice trembling.

The creature grinned. "Jack," he said. "I'm happy for the souls I've damned to hell today."

Bethany's eyes widened. "Why would you do such a thing?"

Jack's smile broadened. "Because it's fun to see humans so easily turn on each other. Watching you destroy one another amuses me."

"How can you get away with it?" Bethany demanded.

"They don't have to listen to me," Jack said lightly. "They can choose not to participate in gossip, hatred, and lies. But when they choose to listen, when they choose to act, they're accountable to God for their actions."

Jack stood there laughing as Bethany and her grandmother stared at him, horrified.

"What do I have to do with any of this?" Bethany asked finally.

"You," Jack said, pointing at her, "are my next assignment."

Bethany's heart pounded. "Assignment?"

"Yes." Jack's eyes gleamed. "Bethany, Jocelyn, her friends—you were all marked for destruction. They took the bait. You didn't."

He laughed again, the sound echoing through the trees, as Bethany and her grandmother stood frozen, unsure if what they were seeing was real.

Bethany began to understand what Jack was telling her. She realized she had been nothing more than a pawn in a demon's game—a game meant to bring as many souls to hell as possible.

"Why?" she asked quietly. "Why did you choose to do it this way?"

Jack's smile never faded. "Because it's subtle," he said. "People hear a whisper, a lie about someone else, and they believe it. From there, the betrayal and hate begin. They feel like victims, convinced they're right in their actions, and from that place of perceived righteousness, they believe they can do no wrong."

Bethany turned back to the necklace she had found—Jocelyn's—and held it tightly. She didn't feel right returning it to Jocelyn's family. Instead, she placed it into a small sackcloth bag and buried it near the well. Somehow, she knew this was what she was meant to do, that it might help someone someday against Jack. It was clear to her now that all of this had happened because people had chosen to listen to him.

I woke up with a jolt. This wasn't just a dream. It felt like a vision from the past. Could it be from God? It had to be. Why else would Jack warn me about any of this?

I got out of bed and realized it was Monday morning. As I dressed for work, I thought about Bethany's Well and made a decision—I would stop by and look around to see if there really was a gold necklace buried there.

Driving to work, I felt groggy and unwell. I prayed as I went, asking for protection and clarity.

The day passed quickly. Alma was glaring at me again—more intensely than usual. I thought to myself, *If Jack is whispering more things to her today than ever, and if she's listening to him, then I need to be on guard now more than ever. Something is brewing with her. I'll find out sooner or later what she and Jack are planning.*

I knew she could tell Jack to go away, but instead she was eating up everything he had to say about me—about how right she supposedly was in her actions toward me.

After work, I caught Alma staring at me again as I got into my car. A chill ran through me. Jack must know I was onto him, and he was planning something to destroy all of us involved in this assignment. But how could he know about my dream? I hadn't told anyone. Could he read minds, too?

I gripped the steering wheel, remembering Alma's expulsion today. It wasn't a coincidence. I knew it now.

I waited for Alma to leave, then drove straight to Bethany's Well. This time, I parked in a different spot from my first visit and brought a trowel for digging. I glanced at the cabin to see if anyone was around. It looked empty. Satisfied, I turned my attention to the well.

I walked to the spot I'd seen in my dream—the exact place where Bethany had buried the necklace. On the right side of the well, I began to dig. The soil was dense, and I dug down quite far before my trowel struck something solid. My heart thudded.

Brushing away the dirt, I uncovered what looked like a sackcloth bag—so old it had decayed into fragile tatters. I tried to lift it carefully, not wanting to destroy it any more than it already was. Setting the clump of dirt and remnants of sackcloth on the ground in front of me, I slowly peeled back the pieces.

There, in the middle, lay the gold heart necklace.

I stared at it, unsure what to do. I wanted to return it to the Cormet estate; it was their property, but I had no idea how.

Then I noticed something else buried with the necklace: a glass jar. Reaching into my bag, I took out the disposable camera I'd brought from work, anticipating I might find something. I snapped a photo of the sackcloth bag as I first uncovered it, another of the necklace, and then another of the jar.

It was small, ridged, and blue—like a Victorian perfume bottle, but unmistakably designed as a poison bottle. Back then, these bottles were made this way to warn anyone who touched them of their contents. This one, though, was unique. It was stamped with a name. Wealthy families often had glassblowers personalize their bottles. This one read: *Simon Owens.*

I had no idea who Simon Owens was, but I knew I would mail the necklace and the bottle to the Cormet estate along with the photographs, documenting the items at each stage of discovery.

From my bag, I took out two clear evidence bags I'd brought from work.

I placed the sackcloth and necklace in one and the bottle in the other. Then I stood up, ready to leave.

That's when I heard it: laughter from the woods.

I froze. It was exactly like the dream. The same laughter. The same place.

But unlike Bethany and her grandmother, I didn't walk toward it. I turned and ran, sprinting back to my car. I threw myself inside, started the engine, and drove as far from Bethany's Well as possible.

I went home and called the Cormet Mansion to find out where to mail the items. The operator gave me a P.O. box address, which I wrote down carefully. Then I drove to the drugstore to pick up a small box and some tissue paper to pack them in. I knew it would be far better and much safer to hand the items over in person, but I had no way to explain any of this—and I certainly didn't want to advertise that I'd taken artifacts from someone's property without permission, even under supernatural circumstances.

After picking up the mailing box, I went home and made dinner. I decided on something quick and easy: spaghetti. Aurelio hovered by my side, nose twitching at the scent of the sauce because it contained hamburger. I cooked him his own hamburger patty, which he devoured before standing there, licking his chops for several moments afterward.

The next day, I went to work feeling tired again. I kept a lookout for Alma, but she was still behaving the same way she had yesterday. I didn't know what to do anymore. I considered telling the crew chief about the issue and asking for a transfer, but I told myself I'd wait until tomorrow. I had too much work to do today. I knew putting it off wasn't smart, but I was afraid of whether the crew chief would take my side—or Alma's.

That afternoon, I found myself thinking about Bethany's Well again. I wondered if people still met in the woods there, the way they had in my dream. I couldn't explain it, but I had a hunch they did.

When I got home, I checked my email and found an unexpected message from Brenda asking to set up a time to talk. I replied that this afternoon would be fine, and told her she could come by the apartment if she wanted.

About thirty minutes later, there was a knock at my door. When I opened it, Brenda was standing there. "I have news for you," she said as she stepped inside. She explained that since I had come here and told her everything I'd learned about Jack and his connection to Bethany's Well, she and her sister had decided to sell Rosario House.

I stepped back, feeling lightheaded. "That wasn't my goal," I said quickly. "I didn't mean to push you into selling the house. I actually like living here—except for the neighbor above me."

"I know," she said softly. "But it's time for me to move on and make a new life for myself. The Rosario House has a strange connection to Jack, anyway. He seems determined to come back.

"I understand," I told her, "but I hope you're not running from Jack. I hope you're selling the place because you want a change, not out of fear."

Brenda blinked, clearly taken aback by my bluntness. Then she composed herself. "I'm not running," she said quietly. "I really do want a change. The bonus is leaving Jack behind."

"Jack is a demon," I said. "And demons are everywhere."

For a moment, I saw defeat creep across her face, but she hid it quickly. "I'll let you know more later, when the house hits the market," she said.

"Thank you for letting me know," I replied. "I'll discuss it with my employer and see what their next steps are."

"That sounds good," she said. She offered me a small smile and then left.

I stood there after the door shut, unsure how to feel. I realized I was going to lose my apartment soon. I had really started to feel at home here. I decided I would let Thomas know about the sale, though I had no idea where that would leave the two of us. What if he decided to stop dating me because of the change? I guessed I would have to wait and see what happened.

I called Thomas and told him what Brenda had said about selling Rosario House. He sounded disappointed, too, but reassured me we would stay together no matter what. I almost believed him when he said it, but I still didn't feel completely confident, and I couldn't explain why.

Later, I gathered everything for the package to the Cormet estate and headed to the post office. I mailed it under "fragile," and the label made me chuckle to myself afterward. On the way back, I stopped by Momma's Kitchen to get my usual meal and a slice of cake. I was trying to kill time before going to Bethany's Well. I figured that if people were gathering in the woods, like in my dream, it would probably be at night anyway. I decided to drive by and see.

I parked at Bethany's Well again and got out. The woods were quiet, the trail to the well dim in the evening light. I walked along nervously, not wanting to stay too long; there was no way I could explain this to anyone if I was caught.

I followed the path deeper until I noticed something up ahead. I froze. In a clearing, a circle of people stood gathered in the deep woods, chanting. Then I heard a spell being cast.

I crouched low, my heart hammering, searching for a place to stay hidden. The scene mirrored my dream exactly. I believed, more than ever, that whatever was happening here—this hidden worship of demonic enti-ties—was what kept Jack tied to this location, rather than Rosario House itself.

I listened for a while longer, waiting to see if the group was still there. They were no longer in a circle, chanting, but standing around talking. I decided it was a good time to slip away undetected.

Then I heard more people approaching, their voices drifting through the trees. Thinking fast, I bent down and acted as though I were looking for mushrooms. It was the only excuse I could come up with on the spot.

The group noticed me stooped over, scanning the ground. One of the women called out, "What are you doing?"

I pretended to be startled and looked up. "Just looking for mushrooms," I said.

She gave me a quick, annoyed look and walked on. I kept my eye on the group as they passed, and in turn, they kept glancing back at me, trying to do it discreetly but clearly suspicious. I had the strong feeling they didn't quite believe me and suspected I might have seen something. I knew I needed to leave as soon as possible.

The group stopped a short distance away, lingering as if deliberately hanging around. Just then, my cell phone rang. I answered immediately—it was the auto repair shop I'd used before to change my oil, calling about scheduling the next one. Seizing the chance, I spoke into the phone as though it were a friend calling.

"That's great," I thundered. "You just got here to help me with the mushroom hunt, and your husband and friends are here to deer hunt."

I turned and looked at the group as I spoke. They heard me and, after a moment, began to leave quickly up the trail toward Bethany's Well.

As soon as they were gone, guilt hit me. I silently repented for lying to God as I made my way back to my car. Perhaps I could have gotten out of the situation without lying. Maybe my lie had shown a lack of faith in God to protect me. A lie was a lie, and in that moment, I felt no better than Trevor. That's what I thought as I walked.

I decided it would have been better not to have come here in the first place, putting myself in a compromised situation and lying to escape it. When I reached my car, I got in and drove home.

That night, I dreamed of being chased by the grey lady in the veil, running through the same woods around Bethany's Well. It struck me as strange to dream of such a thing, especially considering what had happened just the day before.

I woke up to the sound of a female voice calling my name. Opening my eyes, I saw the same grey-veiled lady I had captured in the picture I took at Bethany's Well, along with the images of Jack. She hovered above me, her clothing and veil drifting as though she were suspended in water.

I squeezed my eyes shut. When I opened them again, she was gone. But then I heard her call my name one last time, and a harsh grip clamped down on my left wrist.

I began to pray, asking God to protect me and help me. The presence faded, and I felt she was gone.

I asked God what had happened, and He told me she was a witch using astral projection from the group in the woods. He said they were watching me now to see what I knew about them. God told me they had been fooled into believing Jack cared about them and that they would be rewarded for their deeds against those outside the occult. He told me there were no rewards waiting for them in the afterlife from demons, only deception.

People were only kidding themselves, thinking God didn't see what they did in secret. God knew our hearts and saw everything we did. It was best to live your life with the anticipation that He was with you everywhere—that He was standing in the same room with you.

CHAPTER 15

I stayed back for a little while, but no one else approached me or even looked in my direction. Eventually, I headed back to my car, realizing it hadn't been too smart to come alone. Now I understood, just as Bethany had, how far these people were willing to go to keep their secrets hidden from the community.

When I got home, I couldn't relax. After everything that had happened at work—and then in the woods afterward—my nerves were on edge. I made some tea, but even that didn't help.

A knock sounded at the door. When I opened it, Thomas was standing there. "Do you want to go bowling?" he asked.

I agreed, and we left together. On the way, he noticed how quiet I was. "You seem down," he said. "What's wrong?"

I told him about Jasper, about Alma, and everything that had been happening at work. He looked surprised but listened carefully, then gave a reassuring nod. "We should pray about it when we get back tonight," he suggested.

"That sounds great," I said, feeling some relief as we continued our game of bowling.

I was glad Thomas knew everything now—and even more grateful that he was supportive. Looking at him differently, I began to think we might become serious. He was handsome, with brunette hair and brown eyes, tall, strong, and lean.

When we got back, Thomas walked me to my door. We prayed together about the situation, then talked for a while. Before leaving, he invited me to his Wednesday night church service. "My mother and sister will be there," he said. "I'd like you to meet them."

I smiled. "I'm looking forward to it. And thank you for taking me bowling tonight."

"I'm glad I did," he replied, before saying goodnight.

I went back inside, spent some time with Aurelio, and read the Bible before bed.

The week passed, and by Saturday, I received an email from Brenda. She explained that she had found a buyer for Rosario House and that we would all have to move out by the end of the month. The other residents with year-long leases would have ninety days to find a new place.

I emailed her back, asking why I couldn't stay for ninety days as well. She responded, explaining that since the company was paying my lease, they had already been notified of the situation and were making alternative arrangements for me.

I knew where this was going, and I could already see a hotel room in my future. Looking over at Aurelio, who was happily snoozing on the couch, I wondered how he would handle the adjustment.

I called Thomas and told him what was happening. He said he had just read the email, too. "Don't worry," he reassured me. "Wherever you move, it won't affect our relationship. I hope you'll stay around Boom Town for a while."

Thomas asked me to dinner that night to talk more about the apartments and my job. I agreed, and he suggested we go back to Momma's Kitchen.

"That's my favorite restaurant," I told him.

"I know," he said with a little laugh.

I began to feel a lot closer to Thomas. When we hung up, I felt much better.

I spent the day at home writing and relaxing with Aurelio. Around 4:00

p.m., I started getting ready for the date. At 4:30, Thomas called to say he would be at my place by five.

"That sounds great," I said, finishing up while Aurelio watched me with curious eyes.

Thomas arrived on time, and we headed to dinner. There wasn't much of a wait that night, and we were seated right away—one of the things I loved about living in a small town.

Over dinner, Thomas told me he had spoken with his mother about everything. "She wants to give me one of the family properties to live in for a while," he said.

I raised an eyebrow. "Really?"

"Yeah," he said, a little sheepish. "I've always been against taking money from my family. I've wanted to build my life on my own. But right now, I'm in a pickle—every apartment around here is full."

I nodded sympathetically. "That's tough."

"She offered me the family's small cabin," he continued. "It's actually near your work."

I looked at him in surprise. "Where exactly?"

"It's a small, old—probably historic—cabin right by the old well near your excavation site."

I paused, setting down my fork. "Do you mean Bethany's Well?"

He gave a slight nod. "Yes. But most people don't call it that anymore. Hardly anyone remembers Bethany beyond the old town rumor that she poisoned the well."

I stared at him. "What do you think?"

He hesitated. "I'd hope not," he said at last. "It was my great-great-grand-mother's."

My eyes widened. "Wait—you're descended from Bethany?"

He met my gaze steadily. "It's true. I'm the descendant of the very infamous Bethany."

I felt shocked and asked Thomas what had happened to the family moving to Boston. He gave me a curious look, as if wondering how I knew that kind of detail, but then explained. "The family did move to Boston. Bethany married into an old-money family there. But her parents never sold the cabin here. Honestly, no one wanted it for a long time, with all the tragedy tied to it. I inherited it from my ancestors, and since the property's been maintained over the years, it still stands as a decent house."

Thomas went on to say he wasn't going to wait until the ninety days were up. "I'll be moving out at the end of the month, into the cabin. Later, I'll decide what to do from there."

He asked me if I would come take a look at the cabin soon. I told him I'd love to. We talked through the details for a while longer before heading home and saying goodnight. I had church in the morning, and I was looking forward to it.

The next morning, I made strawberry pancakes and skimmed the Sunday newspaper for coupons and the funnies as usual. This time, though, the front page caught my attention.

The anonymous package I had mailed to the Cormet estate had stirred quite a commotion. The estate confirmed records of the missing necklace with the inscription that matched the one I had found at the well, and the photographs I sent had people talking. But the most significant discovery was the blue poison jar bearing the name "Simon Owens."

The article explained that Owens would have been the future brother-in-law of Rosario House's original owners. It seemed very unlikely Bethany would have had access to either the Owens home or the Rosario home, since both families were close friends of the Cormets.

The article indirectly stated that this evidence exonerated Bethany from accusations of poisoning the well. Jocelyn's necklace and Simon Owens's poison jar had been found together, and while whatever happened that day would likely remain a mystery, the discovery shed new light. Bethany, in fact, had nothing to do with her family's well being poisoned.

I had to admit I felt happy—for Thomas, for Bethany, and for their family—that the truth had finally come out. Boom Town could no longer hold its supposed guilt over them. I was also glad to know Bethany had gone on to live a good life in Boston.

I received a phone call from Thomas. He said he had read the news article. "Did you have anything to do with it?" he asked. "The evidence makes it sound like someone with archaeological knowledge found those artifacts."

"I did," I admitted. "I wanted to return the property to the rightful owner, so I mailed it to the Cormet estate."

Thomas paused. "But how did you even know where to look for the arti-facts—or why to look at all? The well isn't part of the excavation."

"God led me to it," I told him.

He seemed to believe me and, for now, dropped the conversation. "I want to hear the whole story when I introduce you to my family on Wednesday," he said.

I froze a little at that—part surprise, part embarrassment. How was I supposed to explain any of this to Thomas's family? I guessed I would find out soon enough.

Monday morning, I went to work as usual and greeted Christine. I told her about my situation—having to move out of my apartment and probably back into a hotel again for work. She just gave a light shrug and went about her business.

Normally, I wouldn't think much of it. Maybe it was oversharing. But she was always telling me about her problems, constantly portraying herself as a victim. The one time I could have used a real conversation about my own issues, she acted as if it was nothing and walked away.

By the end of the day, I realized she was only interested in having people listen to her. She didn't care about my problems or my life. She avoided me for the rest of the day, and it became clear we didn't have a friendship. She only wanted someone to validate her victimhood, when in reality, it was her own choices that had caused many of her problems all along.

After work, I stopped by the grocery store and spotted Trevor before he saw me. I quickly turned down an aisle to avoid him, hoping he wouldn't notice me. It worked for a while until he finally spotted me and came over to say hello.

I'll admit I was surprised he actually walked over to talk. He told me about his recent experience with his mother reaching out to him after years of estrangement. I had prayed for this: for his mom to apologize for her wrongdoing in the past, and for them to rebuild a relationship.

Trevor told me he had spoken to her but wasn't interested in having a relationship with her. He admitted he could tell she had been going to therapy and had gotten help for the abusive behavior she showed toward him when he was little.

I wasn't entirely sure why he was telling me all of this. Maybe it was God reminding me that He had answered my prayer, and what softened as a result of that prayer was Trevor's choice. He used to be upset about his mom not wanting to be in his life. Now he was upset that she was.

"I wish you the best, Trevor. Take care," I told him, letting him know I needed to get going.

I finished shopping and drove home. On the way, I thought about how I once imagined what life might have been like together. He had told me he wanted to be a psychologist, but when I asked if he planned to return to college to earn his bachelor's degree, he said no. Now I understand why. He had been lying about his life, and I had been so sure I could convince him to want the same future I did. I thought it would work out the way I wanted if I just pushed hard enough.

But you can't make people want the same things you want. And you can't build a relationship with a liar. Trevor's rejection had really been God protecting me from someone who would have pulled me away from Him.

When I arrived home, I looked forward to making dinner and spending time with Aurelio before reading the Bible and praying. I prepared a frozen lasagna, a salad, and a few breadsticks.

As I ate, I thought about what to wear on Wednesday night when I would meet Thomas's family. I pictured black jeans with a sparkly silver blouse. I wanted to make a good impression, so I decided I would also wear my silver heart necklace.

The next morning at work, Christine came over to say good morning. Before long, she was going on about herself and yet another issue she was having. I listened politely for a short while, then excused myself. I no longer felt the need to help her try to solve her problems or listen endlessly. She wasn't a real friend anyway. When I had wanted to talk something over with her, she had made it clear she didn't care.

Later, the crew chief spoke with me about the apartment. Apparently, they would pay rent until the end of the month, and then I would have the choice of moving into a hotel or finding my own place. I thought about it, and finding my own place didn't sound too bad. I decided I would pray about it and also discuss it with Thomas.

Wednesday night arrived, and I got ready. I slipped on the black jeans, the silver blouse, and my silver heart necklace. When Thomas picked me up at my door, he smiled.

"You look beautiful," he said.

"Thank you," I replied, and we headed off to his church.

His mom and sister were already inside when we arrived. As soon as they saw Thomas, they waved. He led me over and said, "Mom, Sarah, this is…" He introduced me, and we all sat down together in the same pew.

His family was lovely. They mostly chatted with Thomas, but they asked me a few questions and made polite small talk. I found myself admiring the sanctuary—it was old brick with stained-glass windows that glowed softly in the evening light.

After the sermon, Thomas suggested, "How about Aurelio's? Mom, I know you've been craving Italian."

His mom smiled. "That sounds perfect."

At the restaurant, I shared, "Funny story—I actually found my cat here and named him Aurelio."

His mom and sister laughed warmly, and the conversation flowed easily through dinner.

Later, Thomas drove me back to my apartment. Before I got out, he turned to me. "They like you. And the fact that Mom wanted to go out to dinner after church, that's a good sign. In a few weeks, she wants to have you over for dinner at the house."

I smiled. "That would be great. I'd really like that."

Everything felt like it was falling into place. My life's direction was finally taking shape, and I trusted God to keep guiding me. I felt content, happy, and at peace in Christ.

The next day at work, my phone rang. "Hey," Jasper said on the other end. "Just wanted to check in. How's life treating you?"

I smiled. "Pretty well. I actually found a cat at Aurelio's, the restaurant. And I met someone… Thomas. I've already met his friends, his mom, and his sister."

"That's great," Jasper said warmly. "I'm happy for you."

"There's one thing, though," I admitted. "I'm losing my apartment at the end of the month. I don't know what I'll do yet, but I'll probably have to stay in a hotel for a while because of work."

"Don't worry," Jasper replied. "Everything will work out. You'll see."

He hesitated, then added, "And… how are things with Alma? At work?"

I sighed. "Nothing's really changed. She's still upset with me. She just hasn't gotten over what happened."

"Yeah, I'm still with the same company," Jasper said over the phone, "but they transferred me to another project. I've been working on a Phase One survey."

"Oh, really?" I asked. "How's that been?"

"It just ended," he said. "They're temporarily reassigning me to your current project for a while."

I hesitated. "Do you… want to come back?"

"Not really," he admitted. "But I don't have a choice. At least not for about a month."

"I don't think it's a good idea for you to come back," I told him quietly. "Honestly, it's not even a good idea for me to keep going back every day. But if I want to be around Thomas, I don't have much of a choice right now."

"You're probably right," Jasper said. "But I need the job, and I won't be there long."

I exhaled slowly. "I saw Alma's family the other day. The way they reacted…"

"What happened?" Jasper asked sharply.

"They were cold. Almost hostile."

He sounded irritated. "They shouldn't react like that. This whole situation should just end already."

"I know," I said softly.

There was a pause, then we said our goodbyes and hung up. As I set my phone down, a powerful, ominous feeling settled over me about Jasper coming back to the project—and working with Alma again. I wished he wouldn't return. I wished I could ask for a different assignment myself, at least for now.

CHAPTER 16

ollowing Monday, on arriving at work, I saw Jasper there. He was in a new unit, chatting with everyone just like before. When he caught sight of me, he waved, and for a moment, I felt a flicker of normalcy.

But across the room, Alma's expression hardened the instant she saw her former friend. She glared at me more intensely than ever, her anger almost palpable.

The day dragged on, and I couldn't wait to go home. During lunch, Derek, our crew chief, came over. "Looks like you'll be moving into the local hotel soon," he said. "Probably in about two weeks."

"That soon?" I asked, my heart sinking.

"Yeah. I'm sorry," he said. "It's just how the company's handling housing right now."

I nodded, feeling sad. I really liked my apartment. "I guess I'll start looking for my own place soon," I said. "I just want to be near Thomas—and have somewhere that's good for Aurelio."

That evening, I went home and saw Thomas in the lobby.

"Hey," he said with a smile. "Want to go out to eat Saturday?"

"That sounds great," I replied.

"Momma's Kitchen at 8 p.m.?"

"Perfect," I said.

He started to walk off, then stopped and turned back as if he'd just remembered something. "If you want, you could stay in the cabin at Bethany's Well for a while until you find your own place. I can stay with my mom temporarily."

"That's an excellent idea," I said, relieved.

He hesitated, then added quickly, "Maybe we can get married soon and live there together," and walked away before I could respond.

Back upstairs, I fixed dinner while Aurelio slept on the couch. I brewed tea and sat watching the news. Out the window, I saw Alma's two friends from work standing in the parking lot. It struck me as odd—they didn't live here. Maybe they were visiting someone, or perhaps the buyer of Rosario's House had started advertising the apartments for rent. If that was the case, I'd be interested myself.

I decided to go outside and ask them if the apartments were being advertised. But as soon as they saw me, they hurried to their car and drove off.

"That's strange," I murmured. "I only had a question." Their sudden flight felt almost guilty, as though they'd been caught doing something wrong.

I went back inside, still unsettled, and kept glancing out the window while the news played. Their behavior was suspicious enough that I picked up my phone and called Thomas.

"I just saw Alma's friends in the parking lot," I told him. "As soon as they saw me, they took off. It felt...off."

"Keep an eye on things," Thomas said firmly. "If something feels wrong, call for help immediately and get away from them. I'll keep an eye on you and Rosario House until you move out."

Friday night, after a long week, I finally fell asleep. Suddenly, I was in a cold, shadowy forest with someone I assumed was Bethany. I saw her from behind, as always, her long black hair flowing over a deep red cloak.

This time she turned, and for the first time her face was visible. She had perfect features, her light blue eyes striking against the black of her hair. She was breathtakingly beautiful. She stared off into the distance for a moment, then suddenly turned her gaze to me.

"Bring a pocket knife today," she said, her voice calm but commanding.

The forest around us erupted into flames. Bethany turned away and walked through the blazing trees unharmed, her cloak trailing behind her. I knew, somehow, that this was the last time I would see her in my dreams.

I woke with a start, sitting up immediately. My heart was racing, and I could almost feel the heat of the fire surrounding me. The words *bring a pocket knife today* echoed in my head.

I lay back down, but my sheets were damp with sweat. Getting up, I went to the kitchen for a drink of water, trying to steady myself.

What pocket knife do I even have? I thought. Then I remembered—I kept one in my work bag. I went to get it, placing it beside my car keys on the counter.

"I must be crazy," I muttered to myself. "This can't be real." But then I thought of the other dreams—Bethany's dreams always carried some truth. Maybe I needed to heed this one, too.

I picked up my phone and called Thomas.

"I had another dream," I told him, my voice low. "Bethany told me to bring a pocket knife today. The forest in the dream was on fire."

There was a pause on the other end. "That's...unexpected," he said finally. "Be cautious today, okay? Just in case."

"I will," I said.

After hanging up, I thought about what to do until it was time for dinner with Thomas. I sat down with my Bible, read for a while, and prayed, the dream still lingering in the back of my mind. Later, I went out to get a few groceries and household items for my last week in the apartment.

I had never seen the inside of the cabin yet, but Thomas had promised to take me on Sunday so we could see what I would need to bring. *It shouldn't be much,* I thought.

I selected a few frozen entrées, some fruit and vegetables, a small bag of rice to go with them, and a couple of steaks for stir-fry. I also picked up more cat food and litter before checking out. When I got home, I put the groceries away, turned on the TV, and watched a movie for a while.

As I sat back down on the couch with a cup of tea, I noticed Alma's two town friends in the parking lot again. The trunk of their car was open, and I could see what looked like a gas can inside.

I'll call Thomas later, I thought. *I'll tell him they're back again.*

Time passed, and I felt a quiet nudge to pray. I did, asking God for protection, especially after the dream I'd had the night before. As I prayed, I heard laughing outside my front door—the same laugh I'd heard before from Jack. This time, it was louder, sharper, sinister.

I started praying harder. *Something could happen,* I thought.

For a moment, I considered leaving for the day, just getting out. But then another thought came. *Maybe that's what they want. Maybe it's cowardly to run. If this is just some game Jack is playing, I won't give him the satisfaction of scaring me.*

I stood up. "No. I'm staying," I muttered to myself.

I decided to make the stir-fry for lunch; it sounded good, and I didn't want to wait until later in the week. By the time I started cooking, it was almost 2 p.m. The late lunch was delicious, and I figured it was fine—I'd be having a late dinner with Thomas anyway.

Then the laughing came again, followed by a knock at the door. My heart thudded. I went to the peephole. No one.

Slowly, I opened the door. A sticky note was stuck to it. *Brenda. Package waiting at the front desk.*

I frowned. "I didn't order anything," I said aloud. "Maybe my parents sent something... or maybe it's work-related."

I slipped on my shoes and headed to the lobby, trying not to overthink it, though it did strike me as odd that Brenda would be here on a Saturday afternoon just waiting for me to pick up a package.

At the front desk, an office chair was turned around, its back facing me.

"Hi, Brenda," I called softly. "I got your note."

The chair slowly turned. It wasn't Brenda. Antonio—one of Alma's friends from work—faced me with a sinister smile.

"I'm glad you came," he said, his voice low and oily.

He could barely fit into the chair, his bulk straining the arms. I started to back away, but as I turned, Marshall, Alma's other friend, was there, blocking the door.

I tried to move around Marshall, but he planted himself firmly in my path.

"Move," I snapped, trying to push past him.

He didn't budge. Before I could try again, something struck me hard on the back of the head. My vision went black.

When I woke, my hands were tied behind my back. The room was dim and empty—Brenda's office, but cleared out. My head throbbed.

The knife, I thought suddenly. *The pocket knife.*

I felt with my fingers. It was still in my pocket. They hadn't taken it. The rope around my wrists wasn't tied very well.

I started working at it, whispering a prayer under my breath. "God, please help me. Please."

The minutes crawled by as I twisted my arms, finally slipping the knife out. Awkwardly, I sawed at the rope until it gave way. I ripped the last strands off and scrambled to my feet, listening at the door.

Footsteps. Voices. I ducked behind the front desk just as someone entered the lobby.

"Marshall," Alma's voice hissed. "Get the gas can ready. We're going to set the lobby on fire with her in the office."

My blood ran cold. They must have assumed the rope was enough to keep me tied. It might have been—if I hadn't had the knife.

I stayed crouched, holding my breath until their voices faded and the coast was clear. Then I bolted, running back to my apartment. I snatched Aurelio up from the couch and hurried into the hallway.

I knocked on Thomas's door—no answer. Heart pounding, I carried Aurelio out to the parking lot. Just as I reached my car, Jasper's truck screeched into the lot.

"Jasper?" I called, momentarily forgetting about escaping. "What are you doing here?"

He jumped out of his truck, looking frantic. "Alma called me. She said you were hurt in the lobby—she told me to get here as fast as I could."

"I just came from the lobby," I said sharply. "Alma's not hurt."

His face went pale. "Then why would she—" He stopped himself, eyes narrowing. "Why would she lie about that?"

"Because," I said, holding his gaze, "I think she's planning on killing both of us. She tried to trap me inside a burning building. That's what the gas can is for."

Jasper stepped back, stunned. "What?"

I held out my arms, showing the rope burns and scrapes. "This is from being tied up in an office chair while Alma, Marshall, and Antonio discussed burning the lobby down."

He stared at the marks, then at Aurelio in my arms.

I didn't explain. Instead, I opened my car door, put Aurelio inside, and turned back to Jasper. "Thomas offered me the cabin at Bethany's Well until I can find my own place," I said quietly.

Jasper's eyes flicked from me to the cat. He didn't say anything, but I knew he understood—that's where I was going.

Suddenly, a blast sounded from the lobby, followed by the faint wail of the fire alarm inside the building. Residents began pouring out through the side door, but only one came out from the lobby. I moved toward the lobby doors and saw three of them struggling to escape through the glass front doors.

Behind me, Jack's laugh echoed—low and unhinged.

"God..." Thomas's voice broke through the chaos. He had arrived and was standing just behind me, staring at the scene in horror. "What's happening?"

I turned to him quickly. "It's Alma," I said, my words trembling as I explained in a few sentences what had happened.

Thomas didn't hesitate. He grabbed a heavy object and tried to smash the glass door, but it didn't budge. We both tried again, harder this time, but nothing worked. It was as if something unseen—something unnatural—was holding the doors closed. Flames licked at the windows, spreading fast, while the three figures remained trapped inside.

Thomas turned to me, his face pale. "I was going to propose to you tonight at the restaurant," he said, his voice tight with urgency. He pulled a small box from his pocket and pressed it into my hands.

I stared at him, shocked. "Why are you giving this to me right now?"

"Because if anything happens to one of us tonight, I want you to know I love you," he said. "I want you to know I wanted to spend the rest of my life with you."

Another boom ripped through the air. The Rosario House burst into full flames, the heat so intense it felt like the ground itself was trembling. Jasper stood nearby, phone pressed to his ear as he called 911. I stared at the burning building, my stomach twisting. I could have been in there. If it hadn't been for God, I would be in Alma's place at that very moment.

Then I heard it again—Jack's deranged laughter, louder than before.

Thomas turned to me quickly. "Go. Go to the cabin. I'll be there soon. I'll let you in. Then you and Aurelio can go to my mom's house tonight."

"I don't want to be alone tonight," I said, my voice cracking.

"You won't be. She understands," Thomas said softly. "You can sleep in the guest room at my mom's. I'll take the couch."

I caught Jasper watching us, his face etched with distress. He cared about both Alma and me, but there were no winners tonight. His eyes stayed fixed on the fire, traumatized and helpless.

I glanced at my car and saw Aurelio staring at me through the back window, terrified. In that instant, I knew I had to leave. I needed to take him somewhere safe. The only safe place I could think of was with God and Thomas.

I looked over at Thomas. He was still gazing at the building, scanning the windows as if there might be someone left inside, maybe trapped in the apartments. My body ached; the soreness and bruising from being tied up were starting to sink in. The reality of how close I had come to dying hit me hard. I whispered a prayer of thanks to God for saving me and begged Him to save Alma, Marshall, and Antonio, too, if it were possible.

The flames raged out of the open door with a heinous vengeance. Through the firelight, I could swear I saw a shadow moving where Alma had been. For a moment, it seemed to gesture, motioning for her to follow, and beneath the roar of the fire, I thought I heard faint laughter. Was Alma being summoned to hell?

Part of me wanted that to be true. I was glad she was dead. But another part of me felt a deep, reluctant sorrow. Helplessly, I stood and watched the flames devour the once-lovely Rosario House.

The heat intensified, pushing against my skin. I began to back away, mesmerized by the fire's terrible beauty and destruction. Suddenly, I felt my right arm pulled back, and an all-too-familiar voice told me to stand back—the fire was spreading.

I turned and saw Jasper. In the pitch black of the night, he was visible only by the glow of the inferno behind him. Our eyes met, and I slowly backed away, pulling myself from the heat as my senses returned. My gaze darted frantically around the scene.

"Leave now," Jasper said firmly. "I'll tell the authorities you weren't here."

I looked at him one last time. "Where will you say I was tonight?"

He glanced away nervously, then back at me. "I'll tell them you were at the cabin."

He held my gaze. "I know it wasn't your fault—what happened. Alma brought all this on herself. I don't want anyone to blame you. They may try to say she gave you a reason to hate her, and that this is what happened. But they're all dead now because of what she did."

I turned and headed toward my car, feeling numb. The only light around me came from the dim glow of the blaze. I found my car, climbed inside, and started the engine. As I drove away, I felt alone, broken, and isolated— just as I had when I arrived months ago. Things had only gotten worse since I came here.

I pulled out onto the main road and had driven for a few minutes when the quickly approaching red flashing lights and deafening siren of a fire truck startled me as it roared past. In that moment, I realized how narrowly I had escaped with my life, how I had left just before anyone could place me at the scene.

As I drove deeper into the night, a grim clarity settled in. I wasn't sorry for what had happened to her. Alma had destroyed herself. She had destroyed all of them. And she had drawn the worst out of me—the side of myself I had always tried to suppress. In many ways, I was more like her than I wanted to admit.

I prayed for the Lord to have mercy on her soul, as well as on mine, for what had happened. Could I ever forgive her for what she had done? Could I forgive myself for sinking to her level? Perhaps now the murmuring and faint laughing would stop—just as it had begun when I first arrived at this place. The place the locals called Bethany's Well.

www.ingramcontent.com/pod-product-compliance
Lightning Source LLC
Chambersburg PA
CBHW051144020726
47501CB00005B/1669